Theophilus Marzials

The Gallery of Pigeons

And Other Poems

Theophilus Marzials

The Gallery of Pigeons
And Other Poems

ISBN/EAN: 9783337158453

Printed in Europe, USA, Canada, Australia, Japan

Cover: Foto ©Andreas Hilbeck / pixelio.de

More available books at **www.hansebooks.com**

THE

GALLERY OF PIGEONS,

AND

OTHER POEMS.

BY

THEO. MARZIALS.

LONDON:

HENRY S. KING & CO.,

65, CORNHILL, AND 12, PATERNOSTER ROW.

1873.

JE DÉDIE MON PREMIER LIVRE

À

THÉODORE AUBANEL,

L'AUTEUR DE " LA MIOUGRANO ENTREDUBERTO,

(" *The Cleft Pomegranate*,")

EN TÉMOIGNAGE D'ADMIRATION ET DE

SYMPATHIE.

A L'AUBE, en plein Printemps, quand l'amandier fleu-
    ronne,
  Quand l'air tiède, embaumé des senteurs du jardin,
  Se berce à la croisée ouverte, où le jasmin
Son plus secret parfum à ton songe abandonne ;
Quand la nature entière, au baiser du matin,
  S'éveille encor rêveuse, et désire et frissonne,
  Dis, n'entends-tu jamais la chanson monotone
D'un jeune oiseau qui passe et qui chante en chemin ?

Il vole aux bois lointains.   Sa note effleure à peine
Ces beaux rêves charmés que caresse l'haleine
  De l'aurore amoureuse, à l'approche du jour.
Et moi, chanteur aussi, je vais où Dieu me mène,
En fredonnant les airs que peut-être à voix pleine
  Je chanterai tantôt au pays de l'amour.

THÉOPHILE MARZIALS.

CONTENTS.

	PAGE
THE GALLERY OF PIGEONS	1
PASSIONATE DOWSABELLA	40
NOCTURNE	60
THE ELEMENT OF HER BEAUTY	66
SPRING	72
A NIGHTPIECE	73
CHÂTELARD	75
GABRIELLE	77
THE ROSE OF THE WORLD	82
A TRAGEDY	85
AN ARABESQUE	88

	PAGE
IN THE TEMPLE OF LOVE	95
LOVE'S MASQUERADES	140
BAGATELLES	149
TRAGEDIES	152
MAJOLICA AND ROCOCO	159
THE ANGEL OF GOD IN THE GARDEN OF DAME PHANTASY	178

GALLERY OF PIGEONS.

(*A CONCEIT.*)

DAME FANCY has a gallery
　Half-open to the garden-breeze ;—
Around it runs a balcony
　Be-set with oleander-trees,
Slender, thick and blossomy.

'Tis all built up aloft—so high,
It seems a bridge across the sky ;
　And down below, in lawns and leas,
　And hills and dales, and plesaunces,
And corn and dingles of golden rye,
　For one wide sweep the rich glebe-land
　Runs dwindling up on either hand
To where the moorland meets the sky.

Around the columns, scroll'd about,—
   I trow a pleasant pictury,—
Is writ whilere how it fell out
That Jove, whom pretty dreams did flout,
   Along a downy cloud did lie ;
And thence in a rosy and golden shower
    His glory shimmer'd adown the sky,
    Where crystal Sangar wanton'd by
Its mossy banks in bud and bower
Of daffodil and bellamour,
    And flower of luce and lovelily ;
And how from out the panting earth
A ruddy grove at one ripe birth
Of almond rods, shot forth in flower,
    Thick with thrushes' melody.

So to your right the gallery thro'
Is pictured water, green and blue,
   With vermeil perch and silver trout
   Flashing and twinkling in and out,
Amid the rushes' quake and quiver,
    That nude a nymph, the gold drops shaking
    Out her hair, is just forsaking,
    Light her step the long reeds breaking,
Fresh i' the flushes of the river.

Eke the while she dons her smock
She coys and coos to a flapping flock
   Of waterfowl, that o'er her head
Have even perch'd on a willow-wand,
   An ibis rose, an ibis red,
A nightingale, a noisy wren,
A silver swan, a hern, a hen,
   That every second stretch their head,
And snatch or trill when tipt and fann'd
By fingers fair of her fondling hand.

And farther down 'tis rare to see
   How all alone, and mad with love,
   She ran right through the ruddy grove
   Of all those almond-rods of Jove,
As every bud on every tree
   Its bobs and kisses closed and made,
   A-dappling her with dancing shade ;
The while she wanton'd here and there,
And mouth'd the fresh, and cull'd the fair,
And flowerëd all her yellow hair,
   And far too blithe to be afraid,
   Within her buoyant bosom laid
A scraggy almond-blossom-rod,
Gay with the greatness of the god,

That in her bosom bloom'd a-new,
And buds and branches tipt and threw,
And swept and swung, below, above
Her 'shevelled head and feet unshod,
Till large with bloom, and light with love,
The margin-murmurings of the grove
Away did seem to swoon and swim;
While rosy from the river's rim
The light dew round her closed and wound,
And winding, writhing, wreathëd round,
And swept the flowers o'er and o'er,
And white her kirtle toy'd and tore,
And through her limbs sharp shivers sent,
And up the hem betript and bore
And blazon'd all her beauty o'er,
And showers of flowers around did pour;
And round and around her in circles went
Wherever yet her fair foot trod,
And soyl'd the fallen flowers to the sod,
And tost and tript in merriment.

If you would all this story see
And all its merry imagery,
Commend you to my lady.   She
Will lead you to her gallery;

And there awhile
Yourselves beguile
Along th' entablatures and see—
A tale more merry can not be.

My Lady (now you must be told)
Within this gallery doth hold,
Imprison'd in a cage of gold,
  Some thousand pigeons—Oh! the pretties!
  (*O my pigeons! O my pretties!*)
  Cooing all their sweet love-ditties
As their white wings flap or fold.

She comes sometimes at dawn of day,—
  Against the golden wires they cling,
  And all their merry matins sing,
  And turn their necks, or preen a wing,
And all their beauty-tricks display,
  And make them meet for journeying.

She opens the door, they fly away!

Some are white, and some dove-grey,
  Some are black as smokëd pearl,

Some fly straight, and others twirl
And turn and tumble along the way.

Hyüeïps, Hyüeïps. Hyüeïps, Oho !
Out, my pretties ! Ho ! my pretties !
Cooing, cooing love and ditties !
Losing you were worst of pities
Ho ! my pets and pretties, Ho !

All the towns are miles below ;
A league alone there lies below
The church and vane, the chimes go,
And clatters and clashes and booms the bell ;
And over the terrace and dingle and dell—
　　　　Ho !
And over the wenches who yawn at the well,
And flutter above their socks and smocks,
And clash their pails and pannikins—Ho !
Over the poplars, all in a row,
A mile below the elm that rocks,
The tips of gold in the golden glow,
And all the roofs and the weather-cocks,
Squeaking and creaking the redder they grow,
As black and long and black—Ho !
The trees their side-long shadows throw,
Ho, Hyüeïps, Hyüeïps, oho ;

Out, my pretties ! Ho, my pretties !
Mad as merry ! how they go !
Zounds and Zephyr ! and how they go !
Over the corn, and over the cocks,
Over the river and over the hill !
Swoop in the fruitery, apple and pear,
Hyüeèps, and up to the tips of the air !
Hyüeèps, and up and over the hill !
And over the swallows that veer in flocks,
Below, believe ! a league below
The hill itself below the mill ;
And merry and merry the sails go,
Round, and round, and wound with the wind,
And all the folks are standing still,
And all the world runs out of mind,
Aud black their shadow flies behind,
Behind, below, below, behind !
A-running, a-running along the hill,
And large along the golden land,
All rose and red in the rising glow,
Ho ! my pets and pretties, Ho !
Out of earshot ! How they go !
And all the reapers, scythe in hand,
Are shouting:—" Ho ! Hyüeèps, O-ho!"
Whirr and winging ! How they go !
Up and up, and dizzying high,

A little cloud in the rosy sky,
And red the sun leaps up, and gold,
And down they swoop, and over the wold,
All in the twinkling of an eye.

———

My mistress mine is light of hand,
    And dainty, fair, and calm of mien ;
    Her head alone bespeaks a queen ;
All things grow trim at her command.
She strews the cage with shining sand,
    And grain and groundsel, gold and green,
And rose and white she twines a band
Of rose-buds, the gold bars between.

She sets a perch for every pretty,
    With crystal water fills each well,
And hums the while soft amoretti,
    With fragrant breath like asphodel ;—
And such sweet wording makes her tongue,
It seems, for Cupid's worship rung,
    It chimed a little silver bell ;
And song drops glibly from her lips
Like from the rose's curling tips
The dew-drop or the honey drips,
    In twinkling pearl and rubicel.

My mistress mine is lithe and tall,
  She motions not, but glides or moves ;
She helps her maids to deck the hall
  With those fair flowers her fancy loves.
In grace she over-tops them all,
And buoyant is her bird-like head,
  And smoother than a turtle-dove's ;
And round about, a loosen'd thread
  Of fresh carnations and red cloves
Is deftly wove and filletëd.
  Her eyes are dark with violet,
And tender, deep, and still withal.
  With sprigs of pinks and mignonette
Her bosom breathes ambrosial ;
  Wherever eke her foot is set,
Her garment as soft music flows
  In harmony of folds, and yet
It madrigals the while she goes.
  And when she stands so slim and tall,
  Enchanting pictures 'gainst the wall
Her very shadow throws.

My lady's heart is blithe and pure ;
  And eke her hand is sweet and fresh ;
The dimples are as blushing rose,

And creamy peach the dainty flesh :
The very dough she fashioneth
    No need of sugar finds, nor wine ;
The flour that flutters on her breath
    Comes strawberry down or bloom of pine ;
And what she kneads to all desire
    She makes so dainty fine,
Mefears t'would lose at mortal fire
    Aromas so divine.

My lady's mind is saintly sweet,
    Methinks it is a virginal
Whereon an angel's fingers fleet
    Forever fly melodial ;
And thus she thinks but heavenly things,
    That 'mid the tranquil of her eyes
    Most sweetly brim and harmonize,
And blend in hues of angel's wings,
    With pensive loves, and sympathies ;
    And like an holy cordial
That music on the living strings,
    And key-board of my heart. and all,
An echo so excites and rings
    That mirth itself must swoon and fall,
    And melt away beyond recall,

So mutely in such musickings,
  So sweetly melancholial.

*   *   *   *

So swift as is my lady's wit,
  And subtle, fanciful and keen,
  Her pretty fingers yet prevene,
And ply before, and flaunt with it.
  I watch her white hand flirt and flit,
As if a hundred, 'long the screen,
  Like coveys of white turtle-doves
That at the roosting time convene,
  And while the needle deftly moves
  'Mid rosy threads, and silks and gold,
  And purples, and a hundred-fold
Of dapper dyes, her white arms lean
Along the frame-like ivory,
And rare as rich fruit, there between,
Her stooping bosoms are just seen
  To lurk and taper, tip and sigh,
Tight from the silk of shimmering green,
  That lighter than the glib sea-rims,—
  When the white sun is wheeling high,—
  Ripples along her perfect limbs.

Straight from apart the broidery bar
  O'er which my lovely lady stoops,

From out a dark grey earthen jar
Where blue moresques engraven are,
A slender lily plant, as far
  As fair her shoulder, starts and droops
Just at the tip its rosy cup,
Whose every petal crinkling up
  With crimson streaks and graceful scoops,
Shakes tremulous with dreamy smells,
And peals in perfumed ritournels.

She sits i'the deepest of the shades
Thrown down by the long colonnades,
  And though the arches and the loops,
  And tracery, the sun-light swoops
In twinkling beams a-down the grades
And marble floor like wash'd with gold;
And warm the air, in the deep cold,
Comes balmy from the garden-glades,
  And citron-jars in rows, and troops
Of myrtle-shrubs, and dwarf granades,
  And peaches green and white and gold,
Walled the bright length of balustrades.

  Beside her singly or in groups
Stand forth and pose her model-maids,
  In undulating fabrics clad,

With lilies 'mid their girded braids.
　　In hand one holds a blossom-spray,
　　And one a patine freak'd with gold,
Another archly turn'd my way
　　Her massy hair at-length doth hold
　　Above her head, like lawns of gold
　　O'er luscious luxury, and whence
The rose-leaf-rains in dis-array
Shredding about her this, that, way
　　Fleck all her draped magnificence.

One, slimly turn'd, her hand doth lay
　　Deftly along her unstrung lute ;
And one, her head thrown back, doth fray
　　And tip her pouting mouth and mute
　　With gold her tapering double flute,
Whereon her fingers coyly stay,
Or motionless pretend to play.
And one thro' round lips red like fruit,
　　Her long white arm's length and relax,
Wets with the twinkling syrup-sips,
Caught in the curvings of her lips
　　The twisted fibre threads of flax
Drawn through her dainty finger-tips,
　　That up and down and flexile play
The bobbin loose about her knee,

The Gallery of Pigeons.

From yellow as a honey-ray,
The spindle poised gracefully
 On her white shoulder, rich to see
 As cream and peaches, and pardè,
So fresh and strangely fair is she
 That tall she stands in full display,
 A Fate, yet fairer than a Fay.

From these my lady, day by day,
 Beside her broidery frame hath wove
What all the gods and girls have done
 Whilere in gallantry and love.
A mighty work that, faith ! shall be
Unfolded at what time with me
Shall please your high-born seigneurie,
Most gentle sir, or kind lady,
 Around my lady's gallery,
And roseries to rove.

———————

I breakfast on her cakes and wine,
 And strengthen'd by her wholesome grace,
My soul nor needs to drink nor dine,
So long my fancy can divine
 Such rich refreshments from her face.
So where her glances mostly fall

I have a care to take my place;
And loll along the outer wall
  On the broad parapets and base,
  Carved clear against the sapphire sky,
One sweep of azure, framed between
  The columns of the gallery,
Against whose florid flutes I lean,
  And let my light foot dangle high
Above the terrace-plots, and green,
And fountains down below; and down
A mile yet farther, moves the town,
  A clockwork thing that hums and crawls
  Above the puppet water-falls,
And mill and river leagues a-down,
A play-thing to the pigmy town.

And all around the pictured land
Lies mapp'd and sloped on either hand,
Up boundless to the green sea-band
  That like a beryl twinkles blue,
  A hundred miles at least, or two,
Where sky and hill and sea and land
  All mingle out beyond the view.

I thrum my mandoline awhile,
  Some glitt'ring songdrops to distil

From out my soul, that in her smile
    Is balm'd and cordial'd to my will.
I plume and point a peacock quill,
Wherewith I set myself to write ;
    Along my hand I lay my cheek,
And dream into the noon-day light ;
    And round about, and slim and sleek,
And cream and pink, and white and dun,
    My fair hounds fondle here and there,
    And yawn and bask in warm the air,
And gambol in the golden sun.

Within my heart's an aviary,
    Where wanton thoughts do pipe and play ;
My pretty loves of Fantasie,
Come stretch your wings, and get you free—
    I open the door—they fly away !

All my pretty thoughts a-twitter,
    Shimmer out in the golden sun,
I' the liquid ether gleam and glitter,
    Swoop in swarm and wing by one.
Gold and green, and cramoisie,
    Bronze and rainbow, rose and blues,
Velvet, violet, vermilly,
Ruby, peach, and pink, and pea,

Pearl, maroon, and sun, in sea,
   Rains of jewels in joyful hues.

Twirling streak, and light'ning ray,
Star and flame, and fountain-spray ;
   Out my pets, and perts, and pretties,
Up, your lyric flights essay !
Shimmering, glimmering, out, away,
Rondel, sonnet, roundelay,
Diamond, jasper, swing and sway,
Dreamily dropt in downs of day,
Sun and sapphire,—out—away !
   Shrilling and trilling in clear concetti,
   Million-mouth'd in amoretti,
Raining rich in rose array,
Farther, farther, out away !
   Rhetoric, and rose, and ditty,
   Nightingales were ne'er so witty ;
   Oh ! my pets, so pert and pretty,
Twitter, glitter, pipe and play,
Out as a rose-spun cloud of spray,
Over and out, and flash'd away.

My lady let her needle fall,
   And flung her fair head back the while,
Till each the echoes of the hall

Mimick'd the music of her smile.
The glib laugh purled from light her lips
In ripe rains like pomegranate-pips
    And rippling founts of œnomel,
And like a rose-bud big with flower,
Or ripe fruit at the garnering hour,
    The mirth her cheeks did swell.

"O poet mine, though indiscreet
    Your fancy flight to let so free,
Mefears at roosting time 'twill be
    A trifle less so fervent fleet,
    Against your soul its wings to beat,
And chorus in your poesy.

"O poet mine, tho' volatile,
    And full of caprice as can be,
Your wanton thoughts to thus beguile
A cycle sooner than a mile,
    From out yourself and me.
If I've nor learnt your lore in vain,
    Nor cull'd your sonnets' herbary,
    Nor known your soul its balm and bane,
And fused it in my sorcery,
    Your poet's pets and perts and pretties—
    (And losing them were worst of pities!)

Mefears will ne'er come back again,
They are so scatter'd, mount and main,
  A thousand miles and out to sea,
And some are lost in years ago,
  And some in years have yet to be ;
And some have soar'd beyond all time,—
Far out of reason, out of rhyme,
  To east and west, above, below,
Beyond eternity.

" And some have flown to a pleach'd pleasaunce
  And swing athwart the fountain-falls,
And lose the poet's read romaunce
  'Mid maddening maze of madrigals.
They flap and trill, and pipe applause ;
  The laughing ladies wave their hands,
And flutter scarves and lace and gauze,
  And chase them with their gay ribànds ;
And ere the sun the garden leaves,
In truth so trite it fain deceives,
  They'll follow suit in gallant bands,
And night amid their lady's eaves.

" And some have sunk to the orchard-close,
  And peck the pippins round and red,
And feast amid the raspberry rows,

C 2

And spoil the queen's pet strawberry-bed.
And now the gard'ner comes that way,
And flings the net, alack-a-day !—
They ne'er have time to swirl away,
    And now they're all imprisonëd.

" And some by night when sups the king
    Beside the comely courtisan
Are spit and turning round the string
(Mefears I set you marvelling)
    Each one a savoury ortolan.

" And one has swoop'd to a diamond-pane
    To peep at what 'twere sin to see.
My Lady Prue comes nooning there,
And turns the casement t'wards the air ;
And takes your sonnet then and there,
    All lief 'twere in her bosom lain
Or liquid lawns about her knee.—
    And ah ! she is so fair, so fair,
    You fain might spend yourself in prayer,
    He'd let her wring his neck, I swear,
And teach him for temerity.

" And some the prince's fool has caught
    To serve within a fancy pie ;

And when the queen the pastry breaks
　Nor doubts the tasty morsel nigh,
They'll all go forth in shrieks and shakes
Amid the comfits, quince, and cakes,
　And dames in terror like to die.

" And some from off the falcon frames
　Have shot sheer up to heaven's height
　To Venus' balmy bosom, bright
With snowy lawns and farthingales ;
　They peck the sparrows nursed therein
　That all to peep and cheep begin
And voice as shrill as nightingales ;—
　And Venus laughs, she can but fain,
And yokes them to a crystal bar ;
At night amid her doves in star
They'll lead along her rosy car,
And bear her where the banquets are
　In Tethys' beautiful domain.

" And some the courtiers catch in cages
　And teach to sing their ladies' names,
　And add fresh fuel to the flames
The flame of love alone assuages ;
And some are ta'en as gifts and gages
　To win fresh œilliads from the dames,—

And balm'd upon their bosoms sweet,
With rose and amber for their meat,
And from their lips the plums to eat,
    'Tis folly's maddest self that blames,
Or can expect them home for ages.

" And some have flown to heaven above,
    'Mid streets of beryls blue and bright,
    Beturreted to left and right,
And flutt'ring free with banderolles ;
They turn the young saints' heads with love,
    (My poet mine, you are too free !)
They chase them each, below, above,—
    Half madden'd by their minstrelsy,—
Thro' garths of crimson gladioles ;
    And, shimmering soft like damoisels,
The angels-swarm in glimmering shoals,
And pin them to their aurioles,
    And mimick back their ritournels.

" And one has tipt a golden pipe
Of those the roses wreathe and stripe,
    And flaps its wihgs, and swings and sings,
Awhile below the fingers fly
On rows of keys of ivory,
    In mingled runs and quaverings.

It shakes its head and crests of blue,
    Mefears it fain must sing its say :
Oh poet mine, my troth is true ;
Mefears we'll sadly have to rue
The time we let yon wanton thro',
    Would teach Saint Cilly how to play !

"O poet mine, O poet mine !
    Mefears ye put me much to shame ;
For some as rashly down decline
    Into a place I dare not name
So scrannel-scraunch'd in whirls of flame.
    And of the others far away,
    Where'er they be I dare not say,
    But lost or dead, or flown astray,
    Or far too happy, lack-a-day !
    My poet, to return your way !"

My lady laughed. She is so fair,
    She can but know it every whit ;
She knows for one kiss of her hair
There's ne'er a saint but fain would dare
Thro' yonder casement to repair,
    Tho' never, never back to flit,
But waste in an eterne despair.
I' faith she yet might clip his wings,

Or cage him as a bird that sings,—
　She is so fair, she is so fair,
The very saints would dare such things
　For one short kiss of her long hair!

My lady laugh'd, and dropp'd her thread,
And reels and bobbin-wheels, and said :—
　"Oh, poet mine, nor thus forlorn,—
　My pets nor need my crumbs nor corn,
They long and love me so instead!
　I prythee search far out away
　Beyond the sun and sunken day,
Upon a gentle Zephyr borne,
　My pets return, a speck of grey,
　They are so far, so far away."

My lady beck'd her courbent hand
　A-thwart the gardens down below,
Where gentle dames, all quaintly clad,
　Were grouping, bending to and fro ;
My lady call'd them by their names
　(Her voice is music, as you know),
" My ladies! leave your garths and games,
　And cups and balls, and games of grace;
My Lady Prue! my Lady May!
At love, or work, or dress, or play,

My pretties flutter back, medames !
  Be ready at the roosting place ;
And bring me buds from bough and bed,
  And beaupots of your choicest roses,
And lupins, wreath'd in gold and red,
  And all your neatest, sweetest posies !
And bring me eke my robe of rose,
  That fits all features of the night ;
For swifter than your sonnet flows
My pets return on liquid light.
Nor swirl to left, nor sway to right.
I know ye, pretties, by your flight !
No birds, I swear, can wing so light !
Behold, behold to your despite,
  A cloud of black, a reek of grey,
They hardly widen to the sight,
  They are so far, so far away,"

      Fleck,
      A speck,
      I' the cloud of gold ;
      Over the wold,
      The rosy wold,
      Over the hill,
      The purple hill,

A growing group !

A swirl, a swoop !

Nearer, nearer, nearing still !

Over the black wood, over the plain,

Over the lake, and the corn, and the grain,

And the long white walls where the gourds are lain :

Nearer, nearer, nearing still,

Mid twilit bloom and purple haze,

Or strips of vines, like chrysophrase

I' the setting sun, and the slanting rays

It sends out straight from off the hill ;

Nearer, nearer, nearing still.

Against the wearying wheels of the mill,

Wearily winging o'er river and rill,

Over the poplar, beyond, below,

Where tearing the torrent is foaming in snow

At foot of the woods in the deep ravine,

And nearer, and over the forest of pine,

And nearer, and nearer, and over the hill,

The goose-girl running along the way,

The cackling geese, and leagues away

Returning reapers : swing and sway,

Down to the barn in a deep decline,

And cattle that low for the milking-shed,

And girls a-calling " Cuds " and " Kitties,"

Through orchards bathed in gold and red;

And over the inn and the hostelry,
The green, and the tennis and trellisëd vine,
And lovers endearing inditing their ditties
Over the cider-butts, over the wine.
Over the host, and the horn on the sign,
Over the porch, and the proud lady
Gone forth in the cool of the even-shine
Along the larches, along the lea;
Then swirl and swoop, and far and free,
And over the bean-slope, black and brown,
And black the shades the shocks throw down,
And ho! and up, and over the town,
(Oho! hyüeèps, hyüeèps, Ohò!)
And over the swallows that veer in flocks,
Below, believe! a league below,
Above the elm, that sways and rocks
The boughs of gold in the golden glow,
And all the roofs and the weather-cocks,
That creek and squeak the greyer they grow
From gold and rose—hyüeèps, Oho!
As black, and long, and black, Oho!
The trees their sidelong shadows throw,
That longer lounge in the light that lingers,
As clatters and clashes and booms the bell,
Rung from the belfry, and, rocking, the ringers
Wave to the wenches, that yawn at the well

And wring up above them their smocks and socks,
And clash their pails and pannikins, Ho!
And titter and splash, and splatter and splutter,
Then flying a-thwart them, flaunt, in a flutter,
Oho! hyüeëps, hyüeëps, Oho!
Zounds! and Zephyr! and how they go!
Swoop and up, hyüeëps! Oho!
A league, hyüeëps! and up, Oho!
And over the terrace, and over the pond,
The cagëd walks, and the lawns beyond,
A-cooing, a-cooing, and love and ditties,
A-flapping and flying. And oh! my pretties!
Indeed your loss were worst of pities!
Ho! hyüeëps! hyüeëps! hyüeëps!
Swoop, and up, to the tips of the air,
Down, and over the gallery stair,
Crowding and crowding here—and there—
I' the crimson streak of the distant sea
The great sun sinks, like a red ruby!

———————

My lady rose, and like the cloud
   That swoons along some wooing wind,
She glided to the gallery's end,
Where steps on steps descend, descend,
   And yet descend, and long'd and lined

The long way down, by carved a crowd
Of gods and girls, and all embough'd
    With boxen shrubs, and glittering eke
With fountain tanks that jar each dye
And mirror'd changes of the sky
    All shot with one long crimson reek
On bronze and blue disharmony;
    And round the rims, with shrilling shriek
    The twinkling peacocks all, that tend
        From terrace flight to terrace flight,
        Are fluttering in the rosy light,
    Where balustrade and buttress bend,
        And arches all the wallèd height
    Rise from the pleasaunce, dizzying high,
    Up to the gallery 'gainst the sky;
    And all so fanciful and light,
        A marvel more than masonry.

My lady stands at top the stair;
    The pigeons swarm up thick as bees,
They flap and flutter everywhere,
    Amid the fruited orange-trees.
Around her shoulders, round her head,
    They cling along the crimson eaves,
And squirrels 'mid the traceries
    And column-heads in carven leaves

Of great trefoil and strawberries,
 And fig-boughs tangled tight in sheaves.

My lady stands at top the stair,
 Against the purples of the sky ;
The dim stars tremble here and there,
The laughters of all nights repair
 To join the loves in either eye.
And round her like elysian mist
O'er limbs too lovely to be kissed,
Just dimly hinted, oh ! so fair,
 Flutters her rosy drapery.

She scatters out the golden grain
 Above, below, and everywhere,
 And long a-down the lowest stair,
And veer'd above the chapel-vane,
To left and right, a-down again,
Again and glittering to the plain,
And leagues a-lounging to the plain,
 And fading, sweeps into the air,
Till all around is largess lain,
And yet runs down in golden rain,
 All thick with pigeons struggling loud,
That coo and flap and squeeze and scold,
 And turn and tumble, crowd and crowd,

Around and around her swept and roll'd ;
   And pitter-patter, Oh ! my Sweet,
   The corn-gems twinkle to her feet,
   And twinkle, tinkle to her feet,
   And glitter, flitter, flutter fleet,
Like Danaë in her shower of gold.

My lady calls them, two by two ;
   (Her voice is music, as you know !)
They flutter half the gallery through,
Amid the myrtles, rose, and yew,
   That sweeten through the twilit blue
   Of arch and shadow light and low,
The shot-grey sky is cleaving to.

My lady holds the golden gate,
   And bids her pretties all therein ;
They bill her hand, their mirth abate,
   And flutter, flitter, flutter in.

My lady locks the golden door,
   " And now, my pets, your vespers sing ;
And now again, and yet once more,
   Then pair and perch for slumbering."

She lays her lips along the bars ;
   The twilight grows a deeper dye.
The purple night gets thick with stars,
   The gall'ry deepens in the sky,
"And now, my pets, your compline sing,
And now to sleep, remembering
The freshest breath the dawn can bring
Must wake me with your carolling."

And now a night-wind steals thereby,
A harmony of every sigh
The sweet souls linger on and die,
   From flowers grown faint with blossoming.

"And now, my pretty ones, good-bye."

My lady sleeps in the northern tower,
   That stands up stark against the night;
On the lofty dial the sleep-crazed hour
   Still creeps along, for the moon is bright.
Above the dial jut out great rings
   Of carven cactus-wreaths in flower ;
And furlongs yet above, to right,
   Against a cornice a griffin clings,

And gnashes and grins in the green moonlight,
　And cringes from slipping the great sheer height,
Down base and buttress, the wall'd rock down,
　Thro' moonlit trail that lazily lies
Along the valley; and leagues a-down,
　The silent river that foams and flies
By slumbering garden and woodland rise,
　The spare vane-spire that points to the skies.
The market squares, where the moonlight lies,
　And the empty ways of the sleeping town.

At the top of the thinnest pinnacle peak,
　Above the griffin, is tightly furl'd
The banderolle, tho' the light cloud-reck
　Is thinning around the standard bar,
And mid the moonlight, all uncurl'd,
　Goes melting out from star to star.

The Pleiades are just o'erhead,
　And shake and twinkle, green and red ;
And all around them lies the world
　Between the distant hills afar,
The distant silver-strip of sea,
　The widening plain, afar, afar,
Where slopes and woods all blended are
　In moonbeams-trailing out afar,

Out luminous to eternity.
And over all, and large and white,
Calm Dian glides along the night.

My lady sleeps in the northern tower,
    And sleeps as only a pure soul can.
'Tis just the death-still midnight hour
When every breath and swooning flower
    Is witch'd by poppy and tulipan.
There's scarce a sound in the silent night
    But a restless kine-bell from distant hills,
And the nightingales in the broad moonlight
    In myriad madrigals of trills
From out the cedars and cypress trees,
That line my lady's pleasaunces,
    Stretched out so many feet below
    In plats and borders as you know,
And sweeps of moonlight and black trees,
And long black shadows straight from these,
    And statues too and marble grades
With strips of silver striped between,
And tinsel'd tank and stirr'd piscine,
    And broad black lines from the colonnades,
    And trembling trees in their deep dark shades,
    Like a soul that sleeps thro' serenades,

And all unconscious, dreams in bars.
And here and there are twinkling stars.

My lady sleeps in the northern tower ;
   The bowery terrace juts below ;
Above all tracery, carven flower,
   And grim gurgoil is her bower-window.
A pane is open ; the moon looks in !
   The moonlight lies on the floor, a sheet
Of molten silver ; large and sweet,
   The cream-rosebuds and jessamine
Are tottering as they peep therein
Along the loops and carven bars ;
And down beneath and soft, and slow,
The fountain jet, in faltering flow,
   Spurts up and tosses into stars,
And sprays up to the window bow
   Sweet draughts, from off the great square jars
Of citron-trees in flower and fruit,
With glow-worms glimmering at the root,
   And shimmering fire-flies, that skim
   Along the brimming fountain-brim,
Meandering in a million mazes,
O'er beds of lush heartease and clove,
Around, around, beneath, above,
   In rapid dart and dreamy swim,

Thro' perfume-laden garden hazes,
And over and back to the terrace-rim.

My lady sleeps in the northern tower,
(Oh, hush ye! hush ye! my pets and pretties!)
In hand she holds a lily flower,
And round her head sweet cherubs lower,
    And satin garments along the floor
    Tremble with pearls as the moon slips o'er;
    And all on tip-toe round her pour
Their silent songs, my pretty dreams,
    With rhymes and rhythms all unstrung,
That mingle with the soft moonbeams,
    And deep'ning odours of dew-drops rung.

Hush ye! hush ye! my pets and pretties,
    They cling to the carvings and crowd the sill,
And rondel, sonnet, and soft love-ditties,
Mingle and murmur, Oh my pretties!
    With faltering fountain, and flowers to fill,
And moonlight, moonlight flooding in,
    And the distant nightingales that trill,
And the cream rose-buds and the jessamine,
    That shake and tremble and silver spill,
As all my pretties peep therein,
    And wanton at their fancies' will.

The Gallery of Pigeons.

My lady sleeps in the northern tower!
   How fair she is she little knows,—
Her slim limbs lissom as lily flower
   When zephyrs seek their night repose ;
My lady holds some mighty charm,
   Her blush-cheek dimpling, cream and rose,
To lie so lightly along her arm,
   And lie so lightly and lie so fair,
   When every fancy would fain repair
   To night amid her braids of hair,
   The tangled rims of her moonshot hair,
In florid tropes and wreath'd concetti,
Mazed in moonlit amoretti.
Hush, my pets, so pert and pretty
(Indeed your loss were more than pity !)
   Flutt'ring at the window there.

How fair she is she little knows,
   Tho' all the saints may hallow'd keep,
Begirt with poppies, wreath'd in rose,
   With pansied wings that fan to sleep
   And scatter silver here and there,
And harmonise her whole repose,
   In cordial opiate drops of prayer,
   And sweeps of rebecks, moonlit strung ;
   She is so fair, she is so fair,

The very saints would fain forget,`
   And melt the moonbeam moats among,
Along her breath like mignonette,
   And arms along the pillow flung.

She little fears who little knows,
   (My pretties, prithee, yet contain!)
Or else would keep her heart more close,
   Nor let so loose the golden chain.
She little fears who little knows,
   My pretties all are piping in,
And passing kiss her bosom eke,
And lips just parting as to speak,
   In laughter dimpling down her chin.

She little fears, who little knows,
   To leave ajar the golden gate;
My pretties all their mirth abate
   And flutter in her soul within;
And where her sweet thoughts caged are,
   They perch and pair and match and mate,
And murmur strange tales from afar,
   Of love and death and woe and win,
   Till all my soul is echo'd in
And all her holies lie ajar.

She little fears who little knows.

To-morrow when the morning comes,
With sweet aubades, and shawms, and drums,
  And tabret, flute, and violin,
  And one by one the birds begin,
  And rosy day is dancing in,
And all the pigeons perch'd below
Caged in her gallery, as you know,
  Get up and peep, and preen their wing,
  And, as she bade them, shrill and sing,
  And make them trim for journeying.
And when she's caught their calls and ditties,
And wakens up to tend her pretties,
  Sheveling out her braids of hair,
  And bare-foot tripping adown the stair,
Her heart within shall wake as loud,
  And all her fancies pipe in pair,
And all my pretty thoughts in crowd
  Go shimmering out to the tip-top air.
And loud with hers shall blend and borrow,
And rhyme Sweet Fantasy—" Good morrow."

PASSIONATE DOWSABELLA.

(*A PASTORAL.*)

———•———

PART I.

Oh ! the red rich honeysuckles,
And the lanes where bindweed buckles
  Long white blossoms to sweet-briar ;
In the copse the blue jay chuckles,
And the cheeping linnet truckles
  To the round songs of the thrush ;
  Where the deep woods lie and hush,
  Green against the sky and lush,
Where a lark is winging higher, higher, higher.

Oh ! the soft sweet June, the month of roses !
Girls, a-binding columbines in posies,
  Stocks and lupins blue in ribbands string ;
Under every elm a shepherd dozes ;
Cold and dark the shade around him closes ;

Else he pipes fond airs to rings of girls,
Wreathing, round him, purple pansies in their golden
    heads of curls—
As the wethers with the ewes in time go wanton gam-
    bolling.

     *   *   *

Dowsabella, Dowsabella, whither are you going?
All alone along the meads where all the kine are lowing;
Round the porch the white rose-buds, their rich cream-
    heads out-blowing
Scents delicious, nod and beck, their fairest sister knowing;
Winding down the long grey grass, where sing the men
    a-mowing,
Winds the downy river on, with water-weeds a-flowing
Round the sedge and yellow flags, and here a rush up-
    growing ;
Willows, too, where warblers swing, and fair flies sleep
    a-going—
Gauzy wings, and gold and blue,—and all so glimmery
    soft is showing—
    Dowsabel, sweet Dowsabel,—
    Prythee, whither are you going ?

    Satin green the girl was dress'd in,
    Shimmering white as the silver soughs

All her thick light hair was tress'd in,
Big with blossom'd lilac boughs ;
  Tangling and weighing her rich dun tresses
Down on the pearl-white rose of her brows.

Eke her kirtle loose a-slide,
Down her rounded lissom side,
Glided from her girdle tied
  T' where her happy step and light
  Hardly trod, but as alight
  Giddy rose-leaves, red and white,
  Dancing to the songs indite
  Of some unseen zephyr sprite
That has lured them from their brambles,
  And their kisses satisfied.

Thus she tripp'd along the sweet
Flowers a-bobbing at her feet,
As to fondle with mouths sweet—
Sweet the white-rose of her feet—
And to nestle in their dimples
  Ere they curtsied her aside.

Dowsabel, sweet Dowsabel,
(She who loved, and loved so well),
Where the white-green fennel-bed

Cast about its films and feathers,
Sighing, laughing, wanderëd.

Green-white mist by love-winds led,
Waving and winding, the light boughs sped
Up to her waist, and up to her head,—
Round her in kisses white-rose-red ;
Deep in her neck with sweet sharp stinging ;
Tickling, up the rose-blood bringing ;
Round her cream-white arms a-clinging ;
Round her, and round her, tight'ning and stringing ;
Green-white, pearl-white, cream-white, rose-white,
Glimmering,
Shimmering ;
White to her flesh the white light springing,
Up the fennel a-flying and flinging,
Tangled and tossing in light sharp tethers ;
While from far so clear came ringing
All the bells of those merry wethers !

Dowsabel, blithe Dowsabel,
Lissom as a lily-bell,
Fresh as sprout of asphodel,
Wander'd through the orchard-closes,
Like a swimming swan that dozes
Down a river red with roses,

White dog-roses,
Cream dog-roses,
Swung and swaying with the swell.

And away from down the distance,
Down the downy dreamy distance,
You could hear the clowns a-calling
   As they piled the scented cocks ;
And the voices and the flapping
From the bleaching ground, and tapping
Of the wenches that were walling
Up the full fruit-boughs from falling,—
Till the air was soft with singing,
Maidens' names, and winds and winging,
Birds, and buds, and kine-bells ringing,
   And the bleatings of the flocks.

And thus Dowsabella stood
In the cool calm orchard-wood ;
And around her, trod and strew'd,
   Cherry-knots anon were falling
That the wanton winds undid ;
And, above, as if 'twere bid,
   Hark ! a mavis kept on calling,
   Through the echoing orchard-land,
Coy the love that from him hid ;—

And thus Dowsabella, dreaming,
Through the fennel-boughs a-gleaming,
   Like a statue took her stand—
And her hair, and the lilac band
Down around her long neck slid.

  Dowsabel, dear Dowsabel,
    What's that dreaming in her eyes,
    Drowsy, deep, such purple eyes,
    Darkling into ecstasies?
      What's that look of maddening hunger,
      As if sharp some quick sting stung her?
Thrilling into cruel throbs, and wrung, and wrung with
   cries
Into agonies delicious, like an aching dream that dies.

      What's that laughter on her lip?
      Till the rose its kisses sip,
        Slides along her rounded chin;
      And the twinkling dimples slip
      Round her smooth mouth half unclose,
      Where one sees the small white rows
        Of her pearl-teeth part within.

    Dowsabella, Dowsabella,
      What's the reason of that shudder,

When the sun so warm doth shine,
And the briar-boughs that twine,
    Bound with bloom, can grow no rudder?
What's that beauty in her face?
    Wild, strange beauty! as, in passion,
Nods her head in giddying grace
    O'er her bosom, flower fashion;
    Oh! her large and coiling grace,
    And the light that lights her face!

Such a light that draws you nearer,
Draws you till you almost fear her;—
    As a bee, that sips some nettle,
    Sucks, a-drowning in the petal,
Death, that living were no dearer.

Oh! 'tis beauty beyond telling
Up thro' all her body welling;—
    Dowsabella, Dowsabella,
Like a bud with blossom swelling.
And her sweet breath, rose and clove,
Ran along her tongue—" _I love,_"
    Like the glowing of rich wine;
And her laughing limbs did twine
Like to blossoms of the pine,
Or as willow-wands incline,

Passionate Dowsabella.

When the chaffinches make love ;
And her fine breast, full of love.
Panted as with every sigh,
'T seem'd her very soul ran by,
Straining to a dulcet cry,
 As was never set to singing,
  Save along a love heart's stringing,
  Struck in silver threads, all ringing,
Music beyond minstrelsy !

Thus did Dowsabella sigh ;
 And her arms along her breast
 Writhed and tighten'd in, and press'd,
Till the wrenching of her hand
Crackled off the light green band,—
 Leapt a tapering bosom out,
 As a blossom curls about
 Till the green bud bursts, and out
Runs the red-white poppy sprout.
Dowsabel ! Oh, Dowsabel !
Methinks she loved him wond'rous well,
For down her bosom, hot and cold
With love and fever, fair to behold,
Fell forth his flower of the marigold—
In stripes of yellow, and brown, and gold.

What was Dowsabella doing
   There in the hot sun of noon ?
Young green pears from the boughs came
    strewing
  All around, a summer too soon;
    Love is sad, and love is gay,
    Love is merry mad alway—
  Dowsabella loved in June !

Dowsabella was waiting a lover ;
   Who can doubt he kept the tryst ?
   Who can doubt her mouth was kiss'd,
Till its beauty rippled o'er ?
   That her bosom-beats grew stronger,
   Till their strength could hold no longer ;
   Beaten out into a lover;
   Up the fennel feathering over,
   Toss'd about, and still above her
   Sang the thrushes, love to lover ;
   Round her swung the drowsy clover,
    Scent and slumber everywhere.
   Dowsabella was so fair,
  Trust me, for a lover there !

Dowsabella, Dowsabella,
  Well she coyed and courted there :

Where the fennel-boughs could cover,
Green and white; and primrose over
  Swung two butterflies in mid-air.

PART II.

THE pears were in the perry;
  The apples froth'd in the cider;
'Twas twilight; loud and merry,
  The circle grew the wider
Around the crackling fire,
Where red the flames leapt higher
To ghost tales that ne'er tire,
When every girl creeps nigher
  To the swain who sits beside her!

It was kissing, it was quaffing
  The bright bubbles on the ale;
And with shrieking, and with laughing,
  As the grandam told the tale,—
And the fold without was bleating,
  As the thin cold clouds fell sleeting;
But the men their maids a-seating
  On their knees, as ripe as sweeting

E

Bit their lips,—their cold arms heating
    With their stalwart flesh and hale.

And anon the rebeck-player
    Scraped a cord to make them mind,
Till the dancers whirl'd the gayer
    Round in rings, like apple-rind,
Hand in hand the comely pair,
Lubin footing with his fair,
As she mouthed a plait of hair,
Strutting here, and curtsying there—
    The calm beauty, Blowselind.

And the red light leapt up, running
    Round the walls, and stair, and store,
And the gaming, and the funning
    At the cider-butts, and, roar!
Up the chimney wriggled red,
Eke the rafters overhead,
Where the mint and sages dead
Rattled to the dancers' tread.
    Leaping lustier from the floor.

Blowselind's a girl to wed,—
    Large, and calm. and white, and red,
Has her suitors by the score;

When the service is well said,
Meet to mate in marriage-bed ;
  Love no less, and love no more,
Though the whole world else were dead,
  Just as placid as before.

Lubin loves her, in love's stead,
  To the pips of her cold core ;
And a-near—and shame to tell—
Dowsabel, poor Dowsabel,
She who loved, and loved so well,
Writhed, as in the fires of hell,
  In the chill draughts of the door.

After summer out of mind !
Calmer lass you'd never find
  Than broad-bosom'd Blowselind !
And the red light kiss'd her o'er,
As her firm step trod the floor ;
And her white throat and cheek red
  Never ruddier than before ;
And a-near, with twisted head,
  Dowsabel, poor Dowsabel,
Writhed beside the door ;
Stiff and still, she might be dead,
But her round lips pouted sore,

And her heart it knock'd so loud,
And her face, as white as shroud,
  Gleam'd anon with passion pale,
As when murky streaks of cloud
  From the ashy moon unveil ;
And her fearful eyes shrink inward,
  And across the silent heaven—
Dark, the looming deathly heaven—
  She glides as with a sail.

And thus Dowsabella glided
From the red light of the firelight,
Shooting crimson, splutt'ring red,
  More and more,
To the green light of the moon-light,
Checker'd by the diamond window,
  Cold and silent 'thwart the floor ;
And the red light and the green light,
  Jarr'd and marr'd her beauty o'er.

And with eyes as wild as witches',
  Without motion t'wards the door,
With her eyes strain'd out behind her,
    Seeming
As if struggling from a dreaming
  Ever lured her on before,

On she writhed without a stagger,
As if some strong hand did drag her
On and on, she knew not whither ;
   Where the green moon-light did pour,
Till again it slided off her
   And then slid along the floor,
Like a shade into the shadow
   As she mingled at the door.

Close to her back thro' the rattling panes
The cold wind blew on her scalding veins ;
   Yet ever, with burning eyes askance,
Where fever dried the torrent-rains,
   She mark'd the circles of the dance,
   And clench'd in time, as in a trance,
Her fair arms cross'd in passion-pains,
   As foot to foot, and hand to hip,
   Her love and her hate went turn and trip,
     Now before, and now behind,
     Now Lubin, now large Blowselind ;
   And without the whirring wind
Squeal'd into her ears—oh pity !
Dowsabel, whilom so pretty,
Struggled out of brain and mind!

And, just hark, the creaking vane

On the silent barn—again
Taps the ivy on the pane ;
And a fire is in her brain,
And her heart thumps at each strain
   Of her throbbing limbs, entwined !

Dowsabel, thus Dowsabel,
  Scorched as in the flames of hell,
Turn'd and tortur'd, tear and twist,
  All her fair lithe lissom body
That whilom had been so kiss'd,
    In the checker'd curtain-blind ;
And a-down the village street,
Through the rafter'd lofts, the sleet
   In the whizzing of the wind,
    Fell and fell.

   From the spire boom'd the bell !

And the snow lay like a sheet,
  And the wind against the window
In her deaf ears whirr'd and whined ;
  And she heard it with the rebeck
And the laugh of Blowselind,
  Lubin coying her with kisses,
And her tresses round them twined—

And her large eyes leapt flame-fire,
And her fair breasts huddled higher ;
And she circled through the doorway,
Some great madness on her mind.

*   *   *   *

Dowsabella, Dowsabella, whither are you going?
Alone along the wintry wilds where biting winds are
  blowing,—
Down the steps, along the fold, where cold the kine are
  lowing,
The white steam rising from the roofs, just red i'the
  windows glowing ;
And out against a thin grey cloud methinks would be
  a-snowing,
The wan white moon her cold sad face so fearfully is
  showing ;
And through the jutting rafters down her cold grim light
  is flowing,—
And only hark the wintry wind how bitterly 'tis blowing.
Dowsabella, Dowsabella, whither are you going?

Across the waste, across the rise, where stands the still
  chapél,
All black and bleak against the sky, and no one booms
  the bell,

But one cold crow, perch'd up aloft, a croaking curse doth
tell.

Across the crinkling fields of snow, across the rounded
wold,
Where three scrag trees upon the crown are crazy with
the cold ;
The cold stars shivering up above seem like to lose their
hold,
And one has fallen—down it swirls—down in a great
cloud fold,—
And breaks a-through, and bursts—'tis gone, like a sad
soul unsoul'd !
And Dowsabella, Dowsabella, fear'st thou not the cold ?

Oh, Dowsabella, turn thee yet ; the dead are in the night!
A shrieking soul went whizzing by, too quick for ear or
sight,—
Up from the deepest ground it ran and writhed to heaven's
height ;
And all the world is cold and bleak, in cold the weird
moonlight ;
And all the loppard-soughs have arms, and wriggle in the
night ;
And every gnarl hath a great face that mocketh thee out-
right ;

Oh! turn thee, Dowsabel; I shrink and sicken with
 affright!
·And, far away, the last red pane is hidden out of sight.

The very stars are turning faint, the lonely moon turns
 white;—
Another spirit, aye, and two, are struggling in their flight,
And rend away within the wind to somewhere in the
 night.
How many spirits are let loose from out their graves to-
 night!
And all the air is green with moon, and all the world
 snow-white!
And Dowsabella's face was wan as ghastliest moonlight!

Dowsabella never shuddered; never stay'd or look'd
 behind;
Ever shrunk, yet ever glided, as if lured on by the wind
To some terrible great furnance that was burning in her
 mind,
Whose flames reflected in her eyes nigh burnt the eye-
 balls blind.

Thus she stole a-down the wastes, all open to the view,
Where all the winds went mocking, mocking, mocking as
 they blew,

And revelled in the empty night—(There, quick another
    flew :—

Another soul ! I saw its shroud ; like thin flame it ran
    through :

I hear its shrieking die away !) and there a crazy crew,

The willows by the river leer. and beckon her thereto ;

Oh' Dowsabella, turn you yet.—some devil thirsts for you!

And down the open stream the crow went chattering as
    it flew.

Dowsabella, through the silence, crackled through the
    crickling sedge :

Shrinking—ever shrinking—huddled downward to the
    water's edge,—

Down the low slope where the rushes. torn and wither'd,
    freeze and shake,

Glittering as her body's writhings through the tanglenesses
    break,

Ever on without a motion. as of some corpse just awake,

And whose eyes 'gin burn with fires that now never shall
    aslake ;

And her fair limbs strain'd as if some stone some dreadful
    writhe did make,

Yet never moved, yet struggle-strain'd, yet still a writhe
    did make,

And down the river slowly float the icy films and flake.

Her tighten'd hair is torn and strangled, straggled through
    her lips,
And round her neck, and round her hand, and lower yet,
    the tips
Run trickling in the stream below, where eke her garment
    dips ;
And on without a murmur, and a wanting in her eyes,
Looking far, and deep, and down, the water's mysteries—
On she shrinks, yet glideth ever,—downward, down. nor
    sound. nor sigh.—
And the waters close above her,
Round and round as if they love her,
And the bubbles ripple by
Along the freezing river, flaking down along the marshy
    plain,
In cold the moonlight streaming, gleaming, flooding in a
    sheet-ice rain ;
And one shriek rings into the night,
Her soul runs shrieking in hell's pain,
Her poor soul in the cold. cold wind, a-melting with its
    pain.

The waters close below, and lounge, and never move again ;
But wind, and wind, and film, and flake, along the silent
    plain,—
And Dowsabella's cry is still—and is she still in pain ?

NOCTURNE.

HE sat at a spinet and play'd.

He play'd—my beautiful soul with the earnest eyes,
My friend !—my soul, if the soul is the part that can rise
To the heights of God, as with wings,—to the greatest
    sublimities.

He sat at a spinet and play'd.

His long firm hands on the music linger'd, and stray'd,
Longingly, lovingly—I—(did he know I was by?)
I sat in the shade,
Away at the window ;—'twas night ; there were stars in
    the sky,
And the lone moon rose, as afraid
To look on the lovers that stay'd
On the terrace below and whisper'd ; and high, up
    high,

The full-leaved trembling trees, deep in the night were
    laid;

And I,

Sitting there in the shade,

Could hear in the distance the hum of the town, and the
    low soft sighs

Of the wind in the trees, and the soothing hushes that
    stray'd

Over the flowers in the garden, that long'd and look'd
    up to the skies

In silence of expectation,—the pause as of one that had
    prayed.

And below in the lounge and the rise

And silent ceaseless tides of the river, some sort of music
    was made,

As it glided along to the moon. In my heart was a
    music likewise,—

And he sat at the spinet and play'd,

My beautiful, beautiful soul, with the earnest eyes.

What was I list'ning to ?   Strange, for it seem'd

There was hardly a sound at all ;

I sat and dream'd and dream'd ;

And music came in like silence, and moonlight was
    there, and a call

From some late thrush in the walk, and the stars, and
    the shadows on all,
And trembling the ivy that clung to the garden-wall,
And murmured some silvery music of silence.—I sat in
    the shade,
While large white films of tranquil moonlight flooded
    the skies,
To far and far down the river.
                       He sat at the spinet and play'd,
My beautiful, beautiful soul, with the earnest eyes.

Crash! what was that? A silence as loud as a crackling
    of thunder!
My friend had but paused in his playing—I started,
    deafen'd with wonder.
Oh! friend, you are friend no longer, the music has come
    to an end!
My dream has rush'd down from heaven, shatter'd as
    nothing can mend;
Shatter'd, and shatter'd, and shatter'd;—and this is the
    end!
You are only the god that I worship'd before—no longer
    the friend!

For your soul seem'd beck'ning to mine; I follow'd I
    knew not why,

Thinking of nothing but following up thro' the clouds and
    the sky,
Up and up,—alone, you and I !

'Twas night in heaven ; and under a sycamine
Casting a broad black shade from the moon, your hands
    on mine,
You let my head to your feet, my beautiful friend
    incline ;
And life had ceased its sorrows, my heart its sighs,
And I lay at rest, and look'd, and read in your earnest
    eyes
Your perfect soul in your perfect face, and drank of your
    sympathies.

It seem'd I might love you—there, just as I would, and
    just as it ought to be,
At your feet, half worship, half fear,—yet for once my
    soul
Was soothed as with balm, with a passionless strange
    satiety
That gulf upon gulf seem'd to roll
Where empty the yearning had been too much for the
    mortal in me —
Yearning at your great greatness, the floods of your soul
    and your heart,

Your mind, that was made for mast'ring on mine, with a
    hunger as if a part
Of myself had been taken to fill up your greatness; and I
Strain'd to replenish the want till my head and my heart
Rung and rung with their hunger, and now I was fill'd,
    and up high
The white moon went overhead thro' the clearness of
    heaven's great skies,
And your hand stroked mine—and I look'd, and was
    fill'd by your earnest eyes.

Crash ! and I ran to the earth—the playing had come to
    an end.
My dream is shatter'd; it seems as if nothing can mend.

In the world we work on and forget, but here in myself,
    as there,
Is the hunger that yearns of your greatness to have but a
    share,
That can never be mine—but in heaven, perhaps, or as
    when I sat in the shade,
Too weary to think of thinking or doubting—the world
    in a restful disguise,
As if there was something existed somewhere that could
    sympathise.
Something somewhere to be found ere the soul quite dies.

And you, on the brink of whose fathomless being my own
    stands ever afraid,
'Sat at the spinet and play'd.

He play'd, my beautiful soul with the earnest eyes !

—

THE ELEMENT OF HER BEAUTY.

THE BIRD.

O SWEET song-bird in the sunlight winging,
   O'er crimson of poppy and yellow of wheat,
The sun springs out as your songs are springing,
   And fain would be singing a song as sweet.
Sweet, sweet singing, and soft with clover
   And thyme beyond number, and murmur of trees ;
And pérfume and pollen a weft winds over,
Trodden by grasshoppers, over and over,
And crickets re-trilling the trills that are over,
   In shimmer of beetles and booming of bees.
Slumbringly sweet, for the vineyards are nooning,
My sweet one and I are a-weary with pruning,
Of sunlight and sunning, and now for the nooning,—
Low in the vine-props, lull'd by the tuning
   Of vine-leaf and tendril,—my head to her knees.

Q curling and creeping leaf-rustles that cover,
The cooler, the closer, from noon that runs over,
My love in her love in the kiss of a lover,
  With soft leaf-light and sun-harmonies.

O sweet song-bird, in our dreams a-winging,
  And drifting the sun and the summer along,
Till slumber is full of the sun, as thy singing
  Is full of the sun, or the sun of thy song;
Till dream'd in our love is the husbandman, Summer,
  Love-sick and sighing, and thou the reed-flute;
He pipes of his loving, as living gets dumber,
And dumber to death, as the sunning and summer,
And day-light, and music of dancing is dumber,
  And all but the frogs in the marshes are mute.
O bird! the sun is the soul of your singing,
That sings of a love you would fain be a-flinging,
And seeking a solace, the blighting but bringing,—
For singing and soul are as knit,—as the clinging
  Of lizard to lizard, where gnarls the vine-root.
But vineyards are chill, where they shook in the summer,
And summer has sunk as your singing grew dumber,
And weary we wander from night the new-comer,
  Our souls love-o'erladen, our shoulders with fruit.
Heavy with honey drones home the rose-hummer—
  Sun thou art darkened—bird thou art mute.

THE TROUT.

O GAY little troutlet, that runs in the river,
  With flicker of silver and ripple of weeds,
And rustle of rushes and larches a-quiver
  On waters that eddy round eddying reeds.
All is a-grey, and the sky's in a glimmer,
A glimmer as ever a sky should be ;
Silvery grey, with a silvery shimmer,
Where shimmers the sun in the hazes a-shimmer,
The shimmer of river, oh ! river a-shimmer,
  That hurries in cataracts on to the sea.
Cool grey trout in the coolness rushing,
From rapid to freshet, where, flashing and flushing,
The waters lap-leap, and break green on us washing
Our white lissom limbs in the roaring and rushing,
  That shatters up beryls, bright-broken by thee.
Tickled and thrilling, we splash the grey glimmer,
And fling it up, kiss it up, brimmer on brimmer,
  Up-rimm'd to our lips, in-mesh'd by the shimmer
Of drip-dropping lilies, 'twere madness to free.

O gay little troutlet, that ran in our laughter,
   Loud as we sported the river along,
Dashing thy darting, and dancing on after,
   Rimming the grey in the silver among.
And dancing and dancing, as when the god's fire
Be-striketh the satyr with fever and chill,
And madly he dances his love off and nigher
Wheels through the whirling bacchantes, and nigher
The ivy-trails tangle the goat-hair the nigher,
   Till life and love-broken the dancer is still.
O troutlet, the wave is the soul of thy gleaming,
And chilly it striketh, and dancing and streaming,
You fling off your grey in the green river gleaming,
And mingle them river and troutlet, a-teeming
   With dancy light sparkles, the heavier till
The bubble-ice barrier draws nigher and nigher,
All dancing is done, save red in the fire
The husk of the chestnut, as, harder and higher,
   The rill is an ice-block, the river a rill :
I sit by the hearth, as the sedges, a sigher,—
   The pool is all silent—trout, thou art still.

THE LADY.

O FAIR one, fair beyond mortal telling!
　O sweet one, sweet that I love so well!
I kiss your hands, and the red they are shelling,
　Pomegranate grains from the golden shell,
Pomegranate blooms in your beautiful tresses,
　I leaf them, and trifle them out of your hair;
I thin the gold tissue, and shred it with kisses,
And toss it up tangling wove-web of gold kisses,
Up this way and that, in the sun, for whose kisses
　A gold gauze dragon-fly swims through the air.
O fair one, fair as never was flower,
O fain would I look, but my eyelids must lower—
So fain would I drink of your golden shower;
Your mouth's a red bud, and your breast a white flower,
　And fain would I tasting forget they are fair;
But so to kiss on in a shower as this is,
Half-knowing, half-cov'ring your beauty with kisses,
Yet cleave as I will it out-rolls from your tresses,
　I'm lost in the glory that floods everywhere.

The Element of her Beauty.

O beauty, beyond all fading and clouding,
  Whose beams through my being in-slide and roll,
Till full is my love of thy beauties a-crowding
  As crowds in my soul-cells, my love to a soul.
A soul so bemingled 'twere soulless to sever,
  With beauty that beats, that I feel as I see
And know it, and thrill with it ever and ever,
Right through me, a soul that is beautiful ever,
With love of thy beauty, a soul that loves ever,
  And loving makes live this beauty of thee.
O dimpled bloom of thy rose-white shoulder,
O love-warm eyes, no year can make colder,
O beautiful soul that can never grow older,
Though budding and ripening sear and off-moulder,
  The shoot and full-flower, while, beauty, in me
You blossom all sweet, to all sense and for ever,
This sense of the soul, for the soul's the sense-giver,
That feels thou art fair, and for ever and ever,
Though still the trout stand in the crinkle-ice river,
The rushes be wither'd, nor chatter, nor shiver,
  The song in the twilight be still with the bee,
I look and live on, for out-loving comes never,
  Thy beauty my soul—and my singing of thee.

SPRING.

I STAND as on the verge of life ; 'tis Spring,
    When springs are welling ere they brim away ;
When waking birds just cheep and shake their wing,
    And clouds come winding in the virgin day.
I look through fruit-boughs fresh with sprout and spray,
    Down loam-hills loosed by shoots where thick dews
        cling,
From out the deep sky night yet dreams away,
    Down lush marsh woods and waters wandering.
I stand between the past and the pursuing,
    Between the dream'd of deed and the undone,
With all the earth on tiptoe for the doing,
    And breathless for the start-word of the sun ;
And dreaming drifts away and big with song
My full heart fails when it should be most strong.

A NIGHTPIECE.

ENDYMION sleeps along the distant hills,
  Calm in the cool clear kissing of the moon,
That all the far deep night with one long loving fills,
  And crystal light,
  And silver shakes and spills,
Where down the smooth sward-slopes a runnel trills
Like green bemolten jewels; and the squills,
  A starting here and there in slender height,
  Tremble like twinkling stars with dew-drop light
Along his neck, where, lost in slumbering,
His sleep-slack finger ever curbs the string,
  And bends his shepherd-hat enclosing tight
  His comely head ; while in the silent night,
    There at his fair foot white
  Just slipt unheeding from his sandal-shoon,
Two blooms on one tall straight narcissus bend to left
      and right,
    White in the silver moon,
    And whisper a love-tune.

Under thy window in the dank grass deep
  I've laid me down a-thinking, love, of thee ;
The slim bell flowers and bending blades around me
    creep,
    And overhead,
  You lie, my love, asleep !
To sleep have I come hither, but to sleep
Unknown to thee or any ; for in trill and cheep
  The nightingales shall sweeter sing instead,
  And calm the moonbeams creep along thy bed,
Till at the window thou shalt take thy stand,
Thy fair face slumbering, leaning on thy hand,
  And all in the calm moon besilvered ;
And gazing in the night, my love, thou'lt shed
Thy beauty in the world's deep drowsihed,
  Flooding the distant hills, the full-leaved tree,
The stream, the wood, the world, the deep sky overhead,
  Till all shall bend and murmur, love, with thee,
    I' the full light, as they sleep,
  Of that calm orb, thy beauty, that can sweep
  Thro' the most secret cells of all deep things, and steep
  Them through and through with love most tranquilly,
    And love, asleep, as yet I sleep,
      In me
      Shall creep
That sweet strange wondrous consciousness of thee.

CHÂTELARD.

A LONG day spent at Châtelard for sketching ;
 A glowing sky above ; another sky
As clear the lake beneath ; towards it stretching
 The vines and long white walls where melons lie.

We set our easels in a small oasis
 Of orchard-shade, and wearied with the glare
Of noon, our eyes sought on each other's faces
 A rest in reading love, no secret there.

And in that love was nothing to remind us
 How we were leaving other things undone,
And Châtelard rose gloomily behind us,
 And cast a broad black shadow from the sun.

The chatty magpies whirl'd into the thickets,
 The deep datura's breath grew over-sweet,
The finches left their trilling to the crickets,
 The glow-worms glimmer'd faintly at our feet.

The yellowing tendrils quiver'd on the trestle,
  The night-wind found a word still to be said,
And made her heedless hands but closer nestle
  In mine—and yet the love was but half-read.

*   *   *   **

A long day spent for sketching!—Who'd discover
  A sketch in those unfinish'd shades and lines?
For now my heart alone can there recover
  The sense of glowing slopes and torrid vines.

O Châtelard! she left me when your orchard
  Grew cold and bare with Summer and the sun,
And death has left my heart all cleft and tortured,
  And stopp'd the loving ere the sketch was done.

GABRIELLE.

A GRIFFIN crouches on an oriel plinth,
    And thence, pale blue,
   As blue wild-hyacinth,
The curtain slopes the open window thro' ;
Rose-white below, full-flower'd azaleas
   Are set by two and two,
    And just above,
   Along a rod of brass,
Two fond dove-grey ring-doves, all day make love,
   And bill, and preen, and coo.

Here she sat calmly in the evening sun,
    And listlessly
   The while, some courtier spun
His great arms round and close against her knee ;
Or stroked her ivory throat and towering neck
   Of cream-rose savoury,

And broad and fresh,
  Till red the carmine fleck
Leap'd in her shoulder like a peach's flesh,
  'Twas kist so cruelly.

Closely he look'd into her beryl-eyes;
    And, broke with love,
  By soft words, and hot sighs
Like philtres, through her calmness sought to move;
But she the while, as one with little care,
  With courbent fingers strove
    To snap the pin
  Of rubies, and let bare
The lawn about her boddice, and therein
  To fondle-fold her dove.

And pouting in the full curves of her lips,
    An agriot red,
  With juice-stain'd finger-tips,
She fawn'd and fondled on its creamy head;
And then she stoop'd, and gracile, kiss'd its beak,
    Yet never one word said,
      The love to ease
    Of him too broke to speak,

Who crushed i' the noisy satin at her knees
His face as in a bed.

At length, when like to any scullion-knave,
 She bid him go ;
 He slunk away, a slave
To every look of hers ; but with a throe
Of love that knit his brow and clench'd his fist,
 And made his brain to glow
  Like wine and fire.
 Then close her hand he kist,
And went, a-cursing this her hard desire,
 Yet fain to please her so.

Once more alone, she rose i' the purple light,
 Tall as a queen,
 With large and lissom height,
And lovely languors in her comely mien,
" Great love," she said, " works evil like great hate ;"
 And laid a glass of green,
  Blown clear with gold
 And blues, athwart a plate
Of rose and opal ; and then slowly told
 Some oozy drug therein.

Then slurred a cherry through, and, from her breast,
    Perked up the head
  Of that fond dove caress'd,
Warm on her flesh, in kisses lately fed ;
And on its beak she toy'd as just before,
    Dangling the fruit, and said :—
      " He loves me so—
  Lest he should love me more—"
Then stroked the bird that flutter'd down, and lo !
    There at her feet lay dead.

With little heed she placed the phials back,
    And closed with care
  The casket, ebon-black,
And chased with ivory sibyls ; comb in hair,
She stood an instant at the window-bar,
    And breath'd the last warm air ;
      Then shut it close
  As rose the evening star
Above the street ; and then the pearl and rose
    Unbraided from her hair.

And all night long beside her lover-bird,
    With plaintive cry,

The sad mate never stirred,
But bill'd his ruffled neck, and like to die,
Heard but her own low grief the echoes keep
   To mock her in reply,
     And like a charm
   To soothe to sweetest sleep,
Her white-rose cheek just dimpling on her arm,
   The lady couch'd thereby.

THE ROSE OF THE WORLD.

SHE has roses rimm'd around her head,
  And wreaths of roses around her throat,
Or creamy, or crimson, or rose-bud red,
  Or white, pure white as the winding float
A-filming along the noon-day sky,
On waifs of wind that wander by
The boughs of roses, she and I
Are courting 'neath so comelily.

There's one red bud that balms her breast,
  Where two bright beetles have made their bed,
In gold and green, and glimmery dress'd,
  For each, the other be-jewellëd :
Where each may dream the self-same thing,
Of folded foot and of winding wing,
And leaves that lock, and cleave and cling,
And drown them too with perfuming.

And swift her bosoms breathe and sigh,
  The while my kisses athwart them stroke
Her fingers around the rose-bud lie,
  And loose and trifle, and scarce awoke,
The leaves their languid locks unclose,
To fingers fresh and fair as those,
The beetles are sliding a-down the rose,—
Aheigh and Ho !—'tis a love that goes.

'Tis just one kiss, and a close, close clinging ;
  And one runs glimmering up to the sky,
And one to her feet is winding and winging,
  And falls in the fallen flowers to die.
Aheigh and alas ! for ever and aye,
The love they loved is lost alway,
And one is on earth and one is away,—
Who knows who cares how far away.

The Angel of Life at the rose-white feet
  Of the Angel of Death may sit ;
Above in the tree of eternity sweet
  The cherubs flutter and chirp and flit ;
And every star is a red-rose shoot,
And God's great sun is the golden fruit,
And the earth is a blown bud nearer the foot,
And the moon is a fallen flower at the root.

The Angel of Death is calm and fair.
  The Angel of Life, who loves her well,
Shall twine a chaplet of stars to her hair.
  The earth is the sweetest to see and to smell.
She'll lay it, the while he woos, to her lip,
The leaves to bite and the honey to sip ;
And fair her trifling finger-tip
I' the crimson core shall slide and slip.

Our loves are laid in the bed of that rose,
  A rose just made for her and me,—
The leaves their languid locks unclose,
  And leave us bare to eternity.
'Tis just one kiss, and all is over—
A lover falling and falling from lover,
And hell is below me and heaven above her,
A-lack-and-a-day and the love is all over.

The Angel of Life has closed his wings,
  The Angel of Death is swathed inside,
A cherub a song of slumber sings,
  And up to heaven her soul shall glide ;
And I am left, a-lack and a-day !
To waste in fire, and weep alway,
And have no hope for ever and aye—
Cycles beyond the judgment-day.

A TRAGEDY.

DEATH !

Plop.

The barges down in the river flop.

Flop, plop,

Above, beneath.

From the slimy branches the grey drips drop,

As they scraggle black on the thin grey sky,

Where the black cloud rack-hackles drizzle and fly

To the oozy waters, that lounge and flop

On the black scrag piles, where the loose cords plop,

As the raw wind whines in the thin tree-top.

Plop, plop.

And scudding by

The boatmen call out hoy ! and hey !

And all is running in water and sky,

And my head shrieks—"Stop,"

And my heart shrieks—"Die."

*   *   *   *   *

My thought is running out of my head ;
My love is running out of my heart ;
My soul runs after, and leaves me as dead,
For my life runs after to catch them—and fled
They are all every one !—and I stand, and start,
At the water that oozes up, plop and plop,
On the barges that flop
      And dizzy me dead.
I might reel and drop.
        Plop
        Dead.

And the shrill wind whines in the thin tree-top.
      Flop, plop.

    *   *   *   *   *

A curse on him.
      Ugh ! yet I knew—I knew—
If a woman is false can a friend be true ?
It was only a lie from beginning to end—
    My Devil—my " Friend "
I had trusted the whole of my living to !
    Ugh ! and I knew !
      Ugh !
So what do I care,
And my head is as empty as air—

I can do,

I can dare,

(Plop, plop,

The barges flop

Drip, drop.)

I can dare, I can dare!

And let myself all run away with my head,

And stop.

Drop

Dead.

Plop, flop.

Plop.

AN ARABESQUE

I was born to be a merchant,
And the merchandise I'd barter
Are my kisses with some beauty,
  On the white mart of her breast;
And a mart, whose architectures,
In their fanciful provoking,
Far out-do the sporting satyrs
'Mid the foliage, apes and parrots,
  Round the old town market-place.

And her bosom!—and to lean me
At my ease like any Persian,
With a long pipe curling round him,
Set with turquoise and gold net-work,
By his rose-confect and sweetmeats,
Piled in azure-pattern'd saucers,
On a mother-o'-pearl table,
In the cool bazaars you read of,
  Somewhere in the white-hot east.

And her laughter, like a fountain,
Shall leap up and run around me,
And her arms, all rose-bud dimples,
Swung about as timed to rebecks,
   Shall off-curtain cool the sun.

And the scents of hemp and poppy,
From the many blossom'd nitches,
Fresh azaleas and red lilies,
Full of scent and deep with slumber,
Set me dreaming dreams delicious
Of this wonderful embossment,
And the world of wanton fancies
   On this bosom, for my mart.

Beat and throb ! all other thinking
Is as distant as the murmur
Of the traffic down the half-light,
Where the white sun, through a crevice,
Streams along the swarthy eunuchs,
With the guttural-tongued strangers,
And the amulets a-jingling
Round the eyes of large-lipp'd women,
Draped and tall, with sliding footsteps,
Like the stir of silent waters,
   When the red fish flash across them.

And the world without is nothing ;
Great hot sun and garish house-tops,
Where the vine-leaves simmer, crackling
'Long grey walls, and dusky whiteness,
Where the half-cloth'd men lie basking,
At all corners—Oh ! 'tis nothing
Hardly thought of, never dreamt of,
In the drowsiness and coolness
Of my mart so savoury scented,
    Spikenard rose and ambergris.

Half-asleep I look—believe me !
I've an eye alive for barter !
On her mouth a luscious fruit-stall
I but clink one coin of kissing,
To get back a feast of peaches,
Ripe rich fruit—Ay ! ripe to bursting
To be bitten, till the kernels,
Snowy white and streak'd with crimson,
    Ice and thrill me back again.

In her eyes' translucent oceans,
Clear blue-purple to all soundings,
I can catch the gleam of opals,
Pearls and many precious jewels
Twinkling, deep, and stones full-colour'd,

Blue and large and purple sapphires
I must fathom for by looking,
Every look a heart-full brimming,
Rich with scintillating treasures,
Dredg'd up from her very being,
Down and deep from secret holies
Man has never seen or heard of;
Till the very strangeness startles,
And I tremble, fear the drowning,
  And up-start again to light.
  :

In her hair's a goodly dowry,
More a mine of wealth exhaustless—
Gold, such gold so rich and yellow—
Orange gold,—and who so skilful
As your merchant here for coining
Rings and jewellery and ear-gems,
  In the fittest filagrees?

Here's an anklet round our ankles,
Round our waists a tighten'd girdle,
Where my fingers still go weaving
Paraments in quaint devices,
As were never seen or heard of
In the chuckling looms of Venice,
Or the shimmery flowery fabric

Fair the Indian maidens broider
With their lotus-blooms and roses
Round their lithe brown limbs to circle,
Smooth, that it were more than madness
    Just to see, nor feel nor fondle.

All these kisses and gold coining
She must change me now for others,
At a usury tremendous—
Thousands every kiss I gave her,
Millions she can never pay me !
Oh ! the sharper, I must have them !
Oh ! the debtor, kissing, kissing !
Still a life of kissing wanted !

Pound of flesh for pound of kisses !
Flesh red-white to kiss and cherish !
All her body milk and roses,
Pine and piment, wine and honey,
Just to sip of and be merry !

But if yet she cannot pay me,
Who knows I may kiss the nearer,
Know and kiss her very soul out,
Find it pure as myrrh and incense

Rolled from out a sullied censor,
That a child without misgiving
  Flings and offers up to God.

Shall I kiss it out for ever,
With such loves as are unholy,
In the air all dissipated,
Spiraling up above the planets,
Winding in their wondrous circles
Up beyond the sun, and higher,
Through the very floors of heaven,
There to writhe, a wailing witness
Of what might have been and was not !
For the beauty that God gave her,
Trick'd and lost in all this kissing,
And the noisiness of traffic,
And the beautiful suggestions,
Of this crafty fair gargoylment,
That surrounds us, rose and foliage,
Blinding, vicious in its beauty,
Round this mart, that is, her bosom,
And this world and all that's in it,
  Drownëd in the sense of flowers.

Shall I leave it? shall I burn it?
That sweet soul of hers ; or take it,

Innocent and pure and childlike,
Here in mine to mingle ever,
Mine so batter'd with such sinning
To make whole as like an angel's,
With a voice to sing in heaven?
Such a song can die? nay, never!
For its singleness and pureness,
When the dross of these my verses,
Dross of Earth and all its beauty,
With my body lieth dead.

IN THE TEMPLE OF LOVE.

A SYMPHONY IN WORDS.

———✦———

Δει δε σε χαιρειν και λυπεισθαι,
Θνητος γαρ ἐφυς.

I had brought my gifts to the Goddess of loves,
The Goddess of roses and turtle-doves,—
Two creamy birds, and cakes of bread,
A dish of roses large and red
To fillet round some victim's head ;
And a comb of the honey of flowers she loves.

And when I had entered the holy place,
And the large-eyed lady of slender grace
Had lain my birds in her balmy breast,
And thanked me with looks the kindliest,
The curtain closed ; and methought I'd rest,
For the white hot noon ran on apace.

So 'neath the marble porch, clear white
As frozen hills, where, up to a height

The carven columns shed down deep
Cold icy shadows, I lay me to sleep ;
And sloped below in a sapphire sweep
As clear as the sky, the sea lay light.

And light as the sea, the thin blue sky
Deepen'd and clear'd to the zenith up high,
　　Pure, and translucent, and blue everywhere,
　　Paling away where sea and air
　　Fainted in one, far out ; and there,
A white sail hung like a butterfly.

And down below, on the long white sand,
Silver'd and lit, the white sea-band
　　Curl'd with scarce the soft zephère,
　　And over the white crag-rocks anear
　　The straggling gourd-plants loll'd, where sheer
They rose from the bay that lounged to the land.

And, high over all, the warm noon-light
Flooded and glistened to left and to right,
　　On the yellow slopes of the vines, and eke
　　The thyme-sweet hills, and a far-off peak,
　　Where gleam'd a temple, and one blue reek,
Like a bloom of a plum, just lay in the light.

And close to my back, from a pillar's plinth,
As blue as a mountain hyacinth,
 The curtain coils, and clear like glass
 The fountain springs, and the fair boys pass
 Thro' rows of red azaleas,
And sprinkle myrrh and terebinth.

And, perch'd on the curtain-rod above,
Dove-grey, two fond ring-doves make love,
 And a priestess below, in her long robe-train,
 Waters the plots of bright vervain
 With a tapering jar, and anon and again
Her long arm lifts to toy with a dove.

'Twas so I lay by the Temple of Love,
 The sun without and the cold within,
Where dove was cooing and calling to dove,
 'Mid scents of the roses, and sistrum din.
The priestess was slender; a hymn to love
 She sang, as she busied the temple within,
And 'mid my dreams I dream'd of love,
 And the song and the scent came drifting in,
And thus I dreamed in the Temple of Love:—

What was it?   Heigh and ho!
 An ear, and a hand, and an eye,

A life breath's ebb and flow,
  And wonder whispering by.
And over our heads to the breeze
Were tossing the tips of the trees,
Till broke on us brighter than these
  The clouds and the crimsoning glow,
And thrilling with throated ease,
In greens and cramoisies,
The crowds of birds sang reveillees
  To the swift boughs sough and sigh ;
The branches were bent with flowers,
  Pomegranates around did lie,
Or crack'd their rinds, and out in showers
  The glittering grains did shimmer and fly,
'Twas trills and fruits, and showers of flowers,
  And running streams thereby.

And up we sprang from the ground,
  For wonder yet widen'd our eyes,
And swooning at sight and sound,
  Our strange breath caught into cries.
For fresh the blown buds blew,
And our feet were fresh in the dew,
And the white winds freshly flew,
  And shimmering winds unwound ;
And nothing we noted or knew,

But round us were roses and rue,
And our soft flesh thrill'd fro' and thro',
   And wilds stretched up to the skies :
And we stood there more than a score,
   Most fair to hearts and eyes,
For some were rich like fruit to the core,
   With soft brown limbs, and lissom thighs,
And some, as the roses the blown-boughs bore,
   Were white in a blush-rose wise.

And each in wonder and fear
   His cringing hands did reach,
And felt us nigh and near,
   Whose strange eyes did beseech,
And found us rose-bud sweet,
And arms, and throats, and feet,
And flush'd with cold and heat,
   And blushing cars to hear ;
Our mouths, like fruits to eat,
We fondled, and found most sweet,
And garlands of large white marguerite,
   We round us, and round did pleach ;
And we shook from the bent-down boughs above
   Rich purple plums and peach,
And our laughter rang and gladden'd the grove,
   As we crush'd the pulps, and parted for each,

And our hearts so stirr'd with sweet soft love,
　　Our glib tongues tuned into speech.

And clinging and cool to our knees
　　The green grass trembled rank,
Where fountains of fleur-de-lis,
　　And lilies, long and lank,
Went lounging to left and to right,
And down in the dim leaf-light,
Where small flowers freaked the sight,
　　Went mazily booming the bees;
And slender and slim to a height,
And crimson and rosy and white,
The grove with flowers was gaily bedight,
　　And budded from beck to bank;
And we laid us around the rills,
　　And found them fresh, and drank,
And broke the pipes of the daffodils,
　　And played and bathed in the fountain-tank,
And the birds sang out in trembles and trills,
　　As the soft boughs sway'd and sank.

Then shifting shimmering thro'
　　The sun-light shot, and lo!
We laugh'd aloud, and knew,
　　Reflected in the flow,

Our flexile forms and fair,
Athwart the dark moss, where
Bright bubbles broke in air,
  And rank pool-grasses grew,
And 'mid my tawny hair
All wind-waved, here and there
And round my white-rose shoulders bare,
  Their loveliness to show,
Some sweet had loosely strung
  Great marigolds in row,
And back my arms aloft I flung,
  In joyaunce thus myself to know,
And up my limbs the crimson sprung
  Red as the rose-buds blow.

And loud and blithe as the birds,
  We gambol'd the groves among,
And strung our thoughts in words,
  More swooning sweet than song,
And subtle as myrrh did move
Some sense in our souls like love,
That on as we wander'd and wove
  Our waists with blossoming girds,
We callëd us " Cluster of Love,"
And " Thrush-voice," " Peach " and " Dove,"
Till fair fond names thrill'd down the grove,

With trills of the birds along ;
   And mingling in measurëd mirth,
     The rich scents savoury-strong,
Came fresh from out the cool crush'd earth,
   With flower and fruit-juice trod of the throng,
And the sweet time bore us along from our birth,
   Nor dream'd we of finding it long.

But the flowers fell fading below,
   And the soft wind sank to a swound,
And the fountain falter'd its flow,
   And the fruit-boughs lounged to the ground,
The air grew thick and hot,
The clusters closed in clot,
Our rose-wreaths came un-knot,
   Our measures broken and slow ;
Thro' stagnant pool and grot
The echoes our calls forgot,
Nor lark nor linnet nor loriot
   Gave ever a song or sound ;
Our hearts were fainting with fears,
   When all so strange we found,
We held our hands to sweep the tears
   That down our dark eyes larged and drown'd,
And time went on like wilds of years,
   And our wearying ways we wound.

And up the height and higher,
  Where roses rarer grew,
We sought, with sad desire,
  For something strange and new ;
Then hand in hand we went
A-down the dark descent,
Thro' rugged rocks and rent,
  And bramble-brakes and briar ;
And footsore, sad, and spent,
The boughs we backward bent,
And on and on our ways we went
  Thro' sombre wilds of yew ;
'Mid tangle thick and thorn,
  The flowers grew faint and few,
The blue pines rose up sheer and shorn,
  And oozed out bitter drops of dew ;
The great spare trunks from bourne to bourne.
  Mazed out beyond the view.

And lo ! of a sudden, in lines
  All deep and straight and high,
Stretch'd flat to the thinning pines
  A great blue sweep of sky ;
We rush'd with a shout where sheer
  The rock scragg'd down and clear
Let the wild world appear

Thro' straggling balaustines ;
Our eyes in thrill and tear
Were dazzled and fill'd with fear,
We groped our hands out there and here,
  Our heads swoon'd round with a cry,
And when we found our sight,
  Oh ! vision of seas snd sky,
And air and rose-clouds fann'd into flight,
  And the soft wind winding along thereby,
And mountain-tips all snow-bedight,
  And the white sun wheeling high.

For myriad miles or more,
  Below us loom'd the plain,
And rolling along to the shore,
  A river clove it in twain ;
A-far the sweeps of sea
Shone green as blue can be,
And, farther than sight can see,
  Went shimmering, shimmering o'er ;
The soft rose-mist ran free,
From river and shore and sea,
And lay in the light or lounged from the lee
  And shimmer'd in showers of rain ;
And rosy from out the showers,
  The dwindling mountain-chain

In easy slopes and tips and towers,
　Went tapering farther than sight could strain,
Down rose-hung rocks and ledges of flowers,
　We gambol'd along to the plain.

And life and light were new,
　And all the world was young ;
The mountain-marshes through
　We leap'd and laugh'd and sung ;
And look'd up at the light
That burn'd so dazzling bright,
And shriek'd when quick our sight
　The white light leap'd into.
The blush rock-roses white
We pluck'd to wreathe and bite —
And, lo ! on our lips from the black thorn blight
　The red blood-drops out-sprung.
Yet on we danced in the noon
　In bands so wildly strung ;
And wept aweary when oversoon
　We fell the foot-bruised flowers among ;
And one sweet dancer lay in a swoon,
　His giddy head so swung.

Yet 'mid the swoon 'twas sweet
　To lie there in the sun,

Till lo ! the great noon heat
  'Gan scorch us everyone;
We cried in cruel pain,
And wander'd forth again
From out the white-bloom plain,
  With weary faltering feet.
Along the left was lain
The white sand, grain by grain,
A sea-bud, and pink conches twain
  Gay tinted by the sun ;
Beyond, on the level sea,
  The wave-lines, one by one,
Came green as far as sight could see,
  With blue the sky all interspun,
And up the sand melodiously
  Their shimmering rims did run.

We went, and lo ! we sank ;
  It lapp'd us to the thigh ;
We bent our heads and drank
  The fresh foams frothing by ;
And every throat grew sore
And parchëd to the core,
Tho' ever round did pour
  Those bitternesses rank.
And thirsting more and more,

We cried " Oh ! cruel shore
That burns as never yet before
   The sun burn'd in the sky."
And then we wander'd out,
   Nor whither knew nor why,
But only long'd to ease the drought
   That made our thirsting souls to sigh,
All hand in hand and twined about
   Each friend to friend so kindlily.

And after many a way
   With mushroom strewn and squill,
We reach'd a red-cliff'd bay
   Where fresh a stream did trill ;
The branches met o'erhead,
With ripe pomegranates red
And large leaves light-bespread
   A-locking out the day.
Athwart the river's bed
Lay many a lotus-head,
And the green stream bubbled up and sped
   And tost them at its will ;
Right quickly in we hied,
   And gladly drank our fill ;
While scarlet birds and stately cried
   Around in scrannel shrieks and shrill,

With water trickling every side
    From every yellow bill.

Right merry did we sing,
    A-chasing them around ;
And each on each did swing
    The creeper trails that bound
The great boughs everywhere
With clusters white and fair,
That each a streak did bear
    Of purple in a ring ;
And high in the leaf-green air
The glimmering midges were,
All gules and green, beyond compare,
    A-shimmering to the ground.
And so we merry made,
    Since what we sought was found ;
And play'd beneath the full rush shade,
    With trails of water-lilies crown'd ;
Each friend to friend, and ne'er dismay'd,
    The wheeling dances wound.

All blue and clear and white,
    For one wide shimmering mile,
The lake lay bright bedight
    With light and lotus isle ;

And long and fair and small,
Its whole length loung'd in a fall
As straight as the blue rush tall,
   Tap'ring beyond our sight.
And, while we sported all
With dance and song and call,
From out the sedge did clank and crawl
   A great green crocodile;
And ere we had time to flee,
   A fair of the merriest smile,
With shrieks that rang right cruelly,
   Was dragg'd in the blackenëd syle,
And his fair red blood by the lotus-tree
   Up-bubbled a weary while.

Right quickly hence we sped,
   Where streams did narrower flow,
And white around were spread
   The desert plains, and Woe !
Our hearts so heavy grew,
That we so little knew
What dreaded thing or new
   Had happen'd to the dead.
From out the sand there flew
A little rill, and two
Tall palms their great black shadows threw—

Their fan-leaves sinking slow :
A lone black crag upon,
  Shrill shriek'd the vulture-crow,
And preen'd its neck, and flapp'd anon
  Most lazily its wings, and lo !
The sun that like the red blood shone,
  The plain's edge dropt below.

'Twas here we laid us down,
  And each on each did near
The white limb nigh the brown
  For cold and grief and fear :
And chilling down the sky,
The cold wet dew crept by ;
The vulture black did fly
  The purple west a-down.
Oh ! bitter did we cry,
A-shuddering sob and sigh,—
For what was it to live, or die
  As died our friend while're ?
Or what was it to be ?
  And see, and feel, and hear?
And everything to find so dree
  We once had found so passing dear ?
That half the world was sand and sea,
  Tho' half did sweet appear ?

That half our hearts was sad,
  That half our hearts were gay;
That eyes with mirth so mad,
  Had eke such tears alway ;
The sea was hot as the sun,
The sun from the sky had run,
The sky from blue grew dun,
  The dun such dew-chills had ;
Or when was life begun ?
Or when should life be done?
Or should the crocodiles, one by one
  Drag us in shrieks away?
What doeth he in death,
  Or song, or dance, or play ?
His sickening soul still hungereth,
  Perchance for sweets whose sours but stay?
Or dieth he beyond all death,
  As the vulture, a dot on the day ?

So to die out for ever and ever,
  Farther and farther away !
Never to sing, never, never,—
  Never to weep, just dying away ;
  Never to hunger or wonder, never ;
  Never to seek or stay,

Never to play with the roses, never;
    Never be stung, just dying away,—
Dying, dying for ever and ever,
    Out with the day!

A mighty yearning swell'd our hearts,
    A biting pain, a great desire;
The sky grew red and black in parts
    With cloven clouds and flakes of fire—
    Vermillion, crimson curls of fire,
    And fiery tongues of blood-red fire,
    That fierced and lick'd up heaven the higher,
And stung us through with deadly smarts;
    And panting wide like jaws that tire
    Yawn'd as to lap us down leaps of fire.

We cried "What power can make us be,
Can make us die and not to be—
A naught that none can know nor see,
Nor hear nor feel, just not to be,
    Nor dying nor desire?"

We tore our hair, and gnaw'd our hands,
    And mouth'd the earth there as we lay;
And writhed about in the thorny sands,
    Writhing to writhe ourselves away;

In the Temple of Love.

And a wild great shriek out-rang to the west,
With clasping of arms and beatings of breast,
And a glib thought ran us through like rest—
    And we could pray !

O crocodiles ! O crocodiles !
    Slide from the slime-grey rocks,
The hot white sands, and the low cool isles
    Where lily with lotus locks.
O crocodiles ! O crocodiles !
    Come up in crawling lazy flocks,
        Where the waste is still,
        And the low-voiced rill
    Runs into life 'neath the palm that rocks.

Here are limbs so brown and white,
    Fair as fruits to eye and tongue ;
Here are who would die with light,
    Life from all their living wrung ;
Here are hearts, whilom so light,
    Heavy with their songs all sung ;
Praying, death be dear or dreary,
We, of life so worn and weary,
    Fain would die your flags among.

The quick blood-bubbles shall froth and fly
   Down with the runnel along to the river,
Down in the lake where the long reeds sigh,
   And shake as ever we crouch and shiver;
Paling away through the red rocks high,
   Lazily out to the sea with the river,—
     Never to hurry, and never to care,
     Only be lost and mingled where
The waves go wandering ever and ever.

Nor pleasure nor pain can the blood-webs know,
   Filming along in the salt sea grey,
Green and blue the greyer they grow,
   Thinning for ever and ever away
Down where the red sun sank, and lo!
   Sinking yet ever and ever away!
Farther and farther they mingle and fall,
Deeper and deeper beyond recall,
   Dimmer and drowning away with day,—
Falling and falling a fathomless fall,
   Dying away,

    *   *   *   *   *

We heard a rustle in the west
   As if of scaléd feet;

In the Temple of Love.

We cried, " Can death be rest ?
    For rest to weary man is meet ! "
We hid our faces deep in earth,
    And through our hearts a fearful mirth
We went fluttering fervent fleet.

With great reluctant eyes,
    Above our arms and hands,
    We peer'd athwart our prostrate bands
    Down all the wilderness of sands,
And horror caught our cries.

O Death, so strangely dread !
    The green-grey ashy skies
Were bloody, streak'd with red,
    And blink'd with greenish eyes ;
And miles along the plain,
    As far as could be seen,
The green-grey mists were lain ;
    And level there between,
Like green on scales of grey,
    Or thin grey shot with green,
The scaly armaments amain
    Came crawling, crawling up this way,
Down all the distance of the plain
    Where all the clammy mists had been,

Till all the distance crawl'd and crawl'd,
   And scaled and glimmer'd slime and green.

O Death, so strangely dread !
   Our wild shrieks rent the skies,
Our long hair floating from the head,
   The great lights flashing from our eyes.
We cried, " It is the approach of death,
   This strangeness that hath brought."
We closed our eyes, and held our breath,
   In fear of what we sought ;
For all the pleasure of life's pain
Came wand'ring through our thoughts again,
Till death, for lack of pain, with pain
   Seemed cruel overfraught.

      *   *   *   *

One,
   Two,
      Three,
The little stars ran out,
   And twinkled on so cheerily,
And sprinkled all the heavens about.
   And some were green, and some were red,

And one was white, and round its head
  The others a merry dance did tread
  (" Because it is so fair," we said)
Till all the sky came twinkling out.

    White,
  Over the black sand-hill,
The large white moon rose into sight,—
The gliding moon in ghastly light,
Till all the desert plain grew white ;
And white the air, and yellow and white,
And shimmering grey, and glimmering white
  That film'd along so soft and still.

The stream ran on all liquid light,
Grey, and yellow, and bright, and white,
    Out of sight
   In the cool grey night,
    All white.

From every bending blade of the palm
  There dropp'd a great clear drop of dew,—
  A drop of moonlight more than dew,—
That slid along our limbs like balm,
  And thrill'd us through.

And, bill to bill,
  On the palm-trees' top,
Two nightingales so full and shrill
    Did trill
Quick songs and glib and dripping drop by drop
Such full rich notes, delicious, thick, and true,
From each round throat a-rushing, running through,
  All note by note
In one long hurry of music spill,
As some pomegranate, at its luscious will,
    Rips
Its crackling rinds, and sprinkles the ripe grains
  In sharp sweet syrup-rains,
Just fit to trickle down your thirsting throats and lips.

O music, thrilling, piercing sweet
  As never was the stars';
That sank into our heavy hearts, all harmonized in bars,
With quick, short throbs of happiness a-thrilling and a-
    moving,
And listening to the nightingales and drinking in their
    loving;
And murmuring deep within ourselves, "Oh ! ever sing
    such singing,
And sing us into nothingness upon your music wing-
    ing !"

High,
High in the deep calm blueness of the skies,
The liquid ocean deepness of the skies,
    The moon did rise ;
The stars, a-panting as with sighs,
Did die out one by one, we knew not in what wise :—
And ever yet, with sweet soft earnest eyes,
The calm pale moon look'd down, and we could sympa
    thise.

    Deep,
    Dreadful drowning deep,
It seem'd as if we clung
    Along our bodies' brim,
      And swung,
      As far below
Some part of us like one wide sea did flow,
Where large full flowers and deep
    Did rock, and creep,
      And swim.

And drowning, drowsying,
Full of some fair new thing,
    Their scent, so swinging sweet,
    From feet to head and downward head to feet,

Did steep,
And sweep
Along our limbs in some soft pleasuring.

And from our hearts, and heads, and heavy eyes,
Each where a closed lid lies,
All thoughts must flee;
Only just there to be
Over the drowning deepness of that sea,
As never was the deepness of the skies—
The deep blue oceans of the midnight skies.

Then from our aching selves we slide and slip
Down on our own sweet selves as lilies drip
Their heads along the leaf where lazy lotus lies.

Slithering, sliding, as the lotus slip,
We slide into ourselves and sink to rest,
Drowsy and drowsiest,—
While from each leaf the little trickles drip,
And cling to us deep down,
Close with the clinging petals, deep and down;
While quick to every little ripple's tip,
The glib ball-bubbles break in many a rim,
And ring,
A-musicking,

Where swim
The lotus beds,
And swing
And sway and fling
This way and that their nodding, nodding,
Drowsy odour-heads.

Yet if, from off ourselves, deep in ourselves we lie,
With lotus-flowers afloat at top of our water-sky,
On blue the sea-bloom beds, beneath the sea-brakes high,
Where pearl-shells chime and sing soft songs so twink-
        lingly,
And great sea-cactus coil so coldly by,
What part of us hath brought with it an eye
        To see
The moonbeams mingling through the green salt sea,
And green the trails and rustles of sea-sedge,
        And fair the star
        That far, far, far
So slowly sinks into the water's edge,—
Not melting in the waves, but drifting through
As we so surely thought its flames could never do?

And we who left our bodies far away,
Up where the ripples underneath did play
Along the reeds a luring roundelay,—

Whence comes this ear?—
That ever still
We hear
The nightingales so clear
And shrill,
Far, far away,
Still singing bill to bill,
As when the world grew still and dead with day.

Just dimly shrills their song so far away,
Farther and farther, it is almost gone,—
And yet, methinks, somewhere they still sing on.

*   *   *   *   *   *

Deep, deep.
Deep in ourselves, so dreadful, drowning deep,
Our bodies far away,—
That part of us that on ourselves doth creep
And sway,
Swung with the sea-blooms on a sea-bloom'd bed,
So charged with blue and red
It cannot lift its weary, weary head
With blossom coils and trails so weightenèd,
We drifted in a wondrous gentle thing,
So fair we could but drown in it and swing—

Nor think, nor know—just drown in it and swing—
　　　Swing, swing
　　So deep, so drowning deep—

*　　　*　　　*　　　*　　　*

　　　Sleep.

Who loosed the light lids from my eyes,
　And pour'd therein clear balms of dew ?
Who was it winding in soft sighs
　My sleep-slack limbs so softly drew
To tuning of low lullabies ?
　　　Was I awake ?
　　　Was I asleep ?
Or dead beneath the glimpse and gleams
　Of waters many fathoms deep ?
Where all my life came drifting through
　(If it be life that only seems).
A thing that nothing can undo
　All drunken with the white moonbeams, —
　　Like lotus flowers along a lake
　　Thrill'd to the stir the waters make,
　　And all asleep, yet all awake,
　And drifting on in dreams.

*　　　*　　　*　　　*

Through pastures pale with poppies,
  That shake and shift in sleep
Their white leaves where the top is
  A green pod ripe to reap,—
Through crimson grove and coppice,
  Azaleas flushed and deep,
And sweeps and wilds of poppies,
  Where waters lounge and leap,
Where rose-wing'd forms are flying
On white winds wan with dying,
And swoon away with sighing
  Down winding ways for sleep ;
And sleep the garner'd crop is,
  And love the flower of sleep.

I wander on for ever ;
  And watch, far out away,
Where showers, that sough and sever,
  Unwind the rose of day ;
Along wan wastes of river,
  And wilds of worlds away,
I watch them work for ever,
  The waters swell and sway.
Somehow, I know 'tis Labour,
And Love who taps the tabor,

And Death is Love's sweet neighbour,
　And pipes their lives away—
Away, and yet for ever
　They cast the grain away.

The fleecy snows are flowing,
　And tumbling down the hills
Where becks of buds are blowing
　In downs of daffodils ;
Long lines of men are sowing
　Full furrows all their fills ;
The rose-lipp'd kine are lowing
　And tread the water-mills ;
The year is just beginning,
Sweet time that sings a-sinning ;
The swallow's song is winning
　O'er Death's, who pipes and trills ;
And floods of flowers are flowing
　Adown the eternal hills.

The grafter's task has ended ;
　The long day verged in June ;
The blue-down'd plum descended
　From boughs bent down o'ersoon ;
Amid the sunset blended,
　The silvery streak of moon

The day has scarcely ended
    From rosy night to noon ;
And Spring has sunk to Summer ;
And Death's sweet voice gets dumber,
For Love, the latest comer,
    Has taken up the tune ;
Yet Death's song ne'er is ended,
    And August treads on June.

The ripe corn waits the reaping ;
    Long level flights of cranes
Sweep past the scythers, sweeping
    The golden wealth of grains :
The time were sweet for sleeping, —
    The hot sun hardly wanes
O'er weary viners heaping
    Along the sweltering plains
The grapes in crimson juices,
Crush'd out for ripe love-uses,
Till piled-up fruit refuses
    The stalwart foot that drains ;
And Love now lies a-sleeping
    To Labour's languid strains.

The orchard trees are rudded ;
    The clouds a-bounding through

In the Temple of Love.

Have filled the vales, and flooded
  Where kine come grazing to;
The cream is caked and crudded,
  And Winter's work's to do;
And Love's cold hand unblooded
  The white flax fingers through;
And Labour fans the fire,
And white frost numbs the nigher,
And Death's voice falters higher
  And pipes his songs anew;
Without the world's unwooded,
  The cold wind whimpers through.

Through pastures pale with poppies,
  That shake and shift in sleep
Their white leaves, where the top is
  A green pod ripe to reap;
Through crimson grove and coppice,
  Azaleas flush'd and deep,
And sweeps and wilds of poppies
  Where waters lounge and leap,—
There rose-wing'd forms are flying
On white winds wan with dying,
That swoon away with sighing
  Down winding ways for sleep,—

And sleep the garner'd crop is,
    And love's the flower of sleep.

＊   ＊   ＊   ＊   ＊

Am I awake, or dead, or dreaming?
The silent moonlight still is streaming;
    The lit stream flashes, and falters fleet!
And tott'ring above from the tip of her noon,
Adown the deep sky the dreaming moon
Is sinking, sinking, as lost in a swoon
    To the nightingale's song that pierces sweet
From the palm-tree's head that nods in sleep,
O'er the prostrate bands lain back in sleep—
            Sleep, sleep,
    Asleep the moonlit sands along;
And my soul sinks on and away in the song,
    Down winding, winding ways for sleep:—
And sleep is the silent sister of song,
    And love is the vision of sleep.

        ＊   ＊   ＊   ＊

        ＊   ＊   ＊   ＊

THE CREATION OF DESIRE.

She sleeps her mouth on mine,
And dreams this dream of mine,

And close her hand in mine
  Grows hot and throbs and leaps ;
And all of her is mine
To cherish and entwine,
Her face and foot are mine,
  And fair her throat that creeps ;
She's mine and more than mine—
  She's all of me—she sleeps.
The bird in slumber on the palm divine,
  Cheeps.

       *   *   *   *

A silence still more silent than the night
  Far in the east.
A wind so slight, it rather seems a light,
  Ceased.

       * *
        *

A lightness somewhere far, far, far away,
  Creeping along the level world of sands
Then a faint primrose streak, whereon pearl-grey
  A pigmy mountain like a shadow stands.

       * *
        *

The sky is liquid violet to the tip
  Tott'ring with sleepy stars ;

The wasted waifs of twilight wind and slip
Across the moon, as troubled waters trip
   Over a trembling plain of purple nenuphars.

* * *

The moon is whiter than a wither'd rose ;
   The east is redder than a rose's core ;
The rose-light gains and goes
   From distant hill and desert shoal to shore.

* * *

The sun is lounging up, a blood-red ball of red,
   On to the desert's ledge, and up the rose-shot sky
Creeps inch by inch, crawling a cubit high,
    Blood-red ;—
And all the wilderness before it spread,
   Miles upon miles,
    Is dead.

* * *

There is a voice of some one weeping
   Far a-down the wastes of sands.—
My friends are weeping, weeping, weeping,
   With faces buried in their hands,
Their wild hair floating in the wind

In the Temple of Love.

Shakes with withered blossom-bands;
Casting not a look behind,
    Away,
    Afar,
Onward through the wailing wind,
  Onward down the dreadful lands, ·
  The shifting stirring deadly lands,
Weeping, ever, far away—
  My eyes with watching strain them blind—
They wander on away, away,
  Out of sight, afar, afar,
Farther, farther—out of mind.

The nightingales have woke, and wing their flight
  Upward, upward, thro' the sky,
    Afar, afar,
Up thro' worlds of blue and out of sight,
  Upward past the latest lingering star,
    Afar :
And now the star
  Has gone,—
And yet methinks somewhere they still sing on.

        * * *

    Who art thou here at my feet?
      Sweet,
      Wake.

Here, take
My heart in your hand—
Break.

Lips that mine unknown have kiss'd in the night,
Cherish'd and curv'd to my own lips' shape ;
Towering throat and the tortuous nape
My hand has fashion'd and framed to my hand ;
Here is your hair in tawny tangles and tight,
Band upon band.
Fettering heart into heart, and your soul has hold
Here to my soul—and the dawn is so clammy and cold.

Speak,—
Who art thou, the new-comer
I love and I hate ?
Art thou life, art thou death,
Thou and I ?
Is it the time to die,
Or to watch and wander and wait
To ever and ever and ever
Beyond eternity ?

Here is my mouth to your mouth like a measure of
fruit,

Here are my eyes to your eyes like a music the soul
  sinks in,
Here is my heart to your voice like a magical flute,
  Or a shell pick'd up where the billows have long
    boom'd in,—
A passionless voice of the cold calm dead and eternal
    froth of the sea,
  The featureless shores, and the fathomless fates, and
    despair of the things that must be.

Here are my arms to your head like an armful of
    passionate flowers,
  Here is my soul to your body as sweet as the sense
    to the rose ;
Here is my life into yours, like the jingle of musical hours,
  Borne thro' the winds of immensity, on, on the wings
    of repose,—
Wafted along to the wandering shore, where the years
    are as waifs from the tree,
And the waves that are breaking are words from the
    dead, and despair of what never can be.

Tear out my lips from your bosom ; and shake out my
    hands from your hair !
  For the phial of love is like wine pour'd out on the
    pulse of the flame ;

Nay, let me consume like the fire snatch'd forth from the
    brand of despair,
  And die out more nothing than nothing, not even a
    notion or name ;
For love is to life, my beloved, as the wild north-winds
    to the sea,
And the calm that must come, is despair of the dead for
    what must, and what never can be.

    Here, who art thou at my feet ?
      Sweet,
     The desert is dead,
   The hot sun swirls overhead,
    The pool has flown out to the sea,
  The palm-tree is dead,
  Death at our feet,—
  Overhead—
  Above and about us, death.
  It is time we were dead.

       * * *

   Here, take
  My heart in your hand—
        Break.

I started, for all my dream had fled.
The sleep is sailing out of my head ;
I rise and stand from the temple's stair,
And stretch my hands in the violet air ;
And look on the world far out, and where
The red sun sinks in the blue sea's bed.

The light rose-mist that lolls from the lee
Trips over the rose-tost tips of the sea,
Along the shingles and shoals of the shore,
The white sea-birds come chattering o'er ;
The wave-rims, running along before
Where skiffs come in and the white foams flee,

Are fawning along up the mariners' feet
Who drag up the prows to the land ; and sweet,
And brown, and smooth with the savoury foam,
They loop up their nets, and saunter home
Along the sands where maidens come
With fruits, and breads of the whitest of wheat.

And farther, loit'ring along behind,
With garments full of the fresh sea-wind,
The girls come back from gathering shells ;
And the wind the fold of their bosom swells,

And waves out their hair with sweet sea-smells,
Till the saffron and pale green bands unbind.

And nearer a-down the vineyard steep,
Where twilit breezes swoon and sweep,
  The singing viners in tapering line,
  Lead home the cream-white garlanded kine
  Streak'd with the juice of the red-crush'd vine,
With feet out of measure and falt'ring with sleep.

The maids are beyond with the tabor and flute,
And poise on their heads the full vats of the fruit,
  And stroll to the press, where treble and high
  The smooth brown youths with slim girt thigh,
  Splatter and trample, and shout thereby,
Thro' red rich pulps resisting the foot.

All over the world is the violet blue
Of the liquid ether, all rose-shot thro';
  And clear beneath, hung down half-way,
  The stars like bright stones shake and sway;
  And high on a rose-reek gauzing away,
The moon's clear strip curls silvering thro'.

And a violet shimmery vapour fills
The vales like a lake; whence the tip-top hills

Rise silver above from their purple bar ;
And the altar fire that reck'd afar,
Now flashes and flames like a great gold star,
And a mirror'd beam on the pale mist spills.

And down at my foot up the craggy stair,
Fair forms i' the twilight, here and there,
   Come bringing birds, and cakes of bread,
   And dishes of roses large and red,
   To fillet around some victim's head,
And sprigs of may for bosom and hair.

And here at the home of the Goddess of Loves,
'Mid ways of myrtles and slumbering groves,
   The holy ladies wander thro',
   Bearing in hand black boughs of yew,
   With garments trailing along the dew,
And soft voice calling the sacred doves.

And just at my back, thro' the curtain'd door,
Deep in the temple the night swoons o'er,
   The youths like shadows wander the same,
   Their lithe limbs lit by the altar flame,
   And scatter the corn by the roosting frame,
And sprinkle the cassia and myrrh as before.

And so I saunter home again,
Passing the girls and the love-sick men,
  Gone up to worship the evening star ;
  And, stepping a-down where the vineyards are,
  I hear their hymn rise up afar,
Then die away on the night-wind's train.

The moon's thin strip now hangs at my feet
And silvers along the wave-lines fleet,
  And now on the hill-top, high above,
  Black to the sky, stands the Temple of Love ;
  The thick stars shaken amid the grove,
Twinkle and twinkle ; and now in the heat,

Clear from the wind, thro' the slumbering town,
I wander, wander wearily down,
  My heart all soothed with a holy peace ;
  For the goddess has given my soul surcease
  Of sad desire ; and wrapt in my fleece
I wander, shuddering wearily down

Thro' silent woods of cypress trees,
Where stars in the tops swarm thick like bees ;
  Thro' olive clumps, and empty space
  Where wild bats whirl in dizzying chase,

I wander on with a certain pace
To the far-off farm; where housed at ease

Around the saffron flames of the fire,
The farm-boys warm and draw the nigher,
With cakes of curds and honey'd wine,
While Chloris, that sweet flame of mine,
Shrilling her double pipe divine,
Leans by the hearth where the flame leaps higher.

For have I not given to the Goddess of Loves,
The Goddess of roses and turtle-doves,
Two creamy birds and cakes of bread,
A dish of roses large and red
To fillet around some victim's head,
And a comb of the honey of flowers she loves?

LOVE'S MASQUERADES.

—•—

LOVE, THE POET.

IN broad brocades, three laughing ladies sat,
  Hand in white hand, and marygold-girt head
  To warm white throat ; their cheeks encrimsonèd ;
And from their lips intent, the waifs of chat
Went twittering o'er the daisied terrace-plat
  Of Love's delights what time they might be wed ;
  Then Love came by the marygold's bright bed
A gay court poet, peacock-plume in hat.

With soft hand feeling down his slender thigh,
  Where dangling hung his deadly chorded lute,
He 'gan recite of Tristram and Yseut :
  For whose sad loves the silenced dames thereby,
In tears forgot their lords long due from chase ;—
And Poesy had stolen all love's space.

LOVE, THE REBUKER.

I.

Out o'er the windings of a dark side-street,
　High in a closely curtain'd balcony,
A lady's lover coil'd about her feet,
　Drawing her mouth to his ; and swooning by
She forced, to still her quick heart's throb and beat,
　His face against her burning throat ; and high
The gold stars glimmer'd in the midnight heat
　Thro' close set citron jars and rosemary.

Then sudden, from the angle of the square,
Clear to the moonlight, through the death-still air
　Love like a wanton cried aloud for hire ;
And struck with bitter loathing of their sin
The lovers wrench'd apart !—I' the room within,
　They heard a stealthy step creep nigher, nigher.

LOVE, THE TRAITOR.

II.

AND there was one came reeling from carouse,
   Hose at his heel, sword trailing through the mire,
   Brawling a drunken song, and all on fire
At ducats filch'd in some low gambling-house;
And hearing Love from habit drone for hire,
   Listless with rose-wreath toppling from her brows,
   Clear from the moonlight, nodding in a drowse
In the deep shade of the Cathedral spire,

He ran and woke her with a scurvy jest,
   And closed her to him; and Love laughed out clear
Her cruel harlot's laugh; and, hugging, press'd
   Her dagger in—and cried : " Thou fool, rot here,
   Who takest love for lust," and soar'd up sheer,
Leaving his life-blood blackening from his breast.

LOVE, THE IDEAL.

At noon when every dame had sought her bed,
  High in an oriel, peacock-plume in hand,
  And mapped beneath her all the varied land,
Dreaming from out her dainty book she read,
Till of a sudden, with a flame-girt head,
  The one she dream'd of, on light pinions fann'd
  Over the sill, did gently swoop and stand
Beside her, quivering for her full mouth's red.

And in his warm god's arms her cheeks so glow'd
  She hardly mark'd how, writ in rose and gold,
Her own life's page was past, and hardly show'd.
  Then with a cry he vanish'd—shivering cold
The night wind swept the corridors ; the bell
Boom'd for one dead, down from the spired chapelle.

LOVE, THE MINSTREL.

In the deep shadows round the fountain-space,
    Clear to the moonlight and the slim jet's tip
Toss'd into silver, and in twinkling chase
    The fireflies swirl'd between, there, hand on hip,
A lover held his lady face to face,
    Breathing sweet words, letting his fingers slip
Thro' moonlight tinsel'd hair; and crushing lace,
    Sheet-flashing satin and the water's dip

Was all the sound.   Then sudden, far away
At some low terrace tank they heard Love play
    His very soul out soft in soothing bars;
And breathless, list'ning, they forgot Love's time
Was pulsing out from distant chime to chime;—
    And instant day shook out the violet stars.

LOVE, THE DECEIVER.

Deep in a drafty orchard just in shoot,
  A-shivering as the light wind laugh'd and sped,
A soft-limb'd stripling wept and shrill'd his flute,
  With daffodils bound doubly round his head,
" *Why then so woebegone, fair friend ?* " I said,
  " *Now every man some maiden finds to suit.*
" *Come, learn a strain more gaily gamutëd,*
  " *And don some flower can bring forth likelier fruit.*"

" *Not so,*" quoth he.   " *Love came in lady's guise,*
  " *Crimson with sweet intent, and piled our bed;*
" *And when I drew her t'wards it in love's-wise,*
  " *Love laugh'd and spann'd his flaming wings and fled.*

" *Deceived in Love himself, all love is vain,*
  " *And life undone ;* "—and here he wept again.

L

LOVE, THE INTIMIDATOR.

BESIDE a fountain's spurting trumpeter
  A large white-throated lady lean'd and flung
Her long-sleeved arms above her dulcimer,
  And quick the glib notes ran along her tongue,
Like rose and fruit. "*Ah bitter love!*" she sung;
  Then lustily: "*Sweet Death, the comforter!*"
It chanced that Love, the garden slopes among,
  Came like the palmer, Death, and look'd at her.

The lady swoon'd amid her stiff brocades,
  And wept amain, though Love laugh'd low and sweet.
She call'd on Love, but Love with rapid feet
  Pass'd out amid the sombre laurel-shades,
Unto the chamber of her nooning maids,
  And bade them broider at her winding-sheet.

THE GHOST OF LOVE.

THE wan witch at the creepy midnight hour,
  When the wild moon was flying to its full,
Went huddling round a damnëd convent's tower,
  From out the crumbling slabs or tombs to pull
Some lecherous leaf or shrieking mandrake-flower.
  Beneath she heard the dead men's voices dull;
Around she felt the cold souls creep and cower;
  In hand she held a grinning damnëd's skull!

Then through the ruin'd cloisters, strangely white,
  T'wards the struck moon, all swathed in cold grave-
      bands,
  She saw dead Love wringing his hollow hands,
And gliding grimmer than a dank tomb-light.

And with a shriek she rush'd across his path—
And now the hell-worm all her body hath!

LOVE, THE AWAKENER.

Love, through the stars, swoop'd down the violet sky;
  His flaming feet caught at a fountain-brim;
  And crouching there, sweet taper limb to limb,
He stood his rebeck on his moonlit thigh,
Toss'd back his pinions, wreath'd in pansied rim,
  Shaking off silver, and stroked out thereby
  His twinkling strings to swooning harmony;
And tinseling sprays the fountain spill'd on him.

Anear, through a low window left unclose,
The sound stole on through breathing trails of rose,
  And kiss'd the sleeping courtier's comely head;
Who, starting up, felt all his soul on fire,
Rack'd and rent back by some sad strange desire,
  And sleep for ever banish'd from his bed.

BAGATELLES.

The wanton bee that suck'd the rose
  Has loved a leaf away ;
The love that in my bosom glows
  Must stay, and stay, and stay.

And when the rose began to die,
  The bee ran up away ;
But Kitty in my love shall lie
  Beyond the dying day.

For Kitty has a golden head
  As never stood on stalk or stem,
Nor Solomon's seal so dainty set,
  Nor burning star of Bethlehem,

And Solomon's in the strange old story,
  And Bethlehem's in the new,
And Kitty in her golden glory
  Is my religion too.

Bagatelles.

I'd like to be the lavender
   That makes her linen sweet,
And swoon and sweeten in her breast,
   And faint around her feet.

She'd hardly think of me at all,
   And shake out lawn and sheet ;
And yet I'd be the lavender,
   And make her linen sweet.

To you who have no thought of God,
   What fear is there of thunder ?
And you who never saw her face,
   What want of love or wonder ?

For like as lightning strikes one dead
   To clangs of God's cithole,
Her face so rose-bud rare and red
   Strikes life into my soul !

CHELSEA.

AND life is like a pipe,
  And love is the fusee ;
The pipe draws well, but bar the light,
  And what's the use to me ?

So light it up, and puff away
  An empty morning through,
And when it's out—why love is out,
  And life's as well out too !

THE lords of state, and the thieving sparrows,
  Have settled noisily back to town ;
The girls with flowers and shrill calabrians
  Drone in the distance, up and down.

I cannot write, or read, or practise ;
  I sit and grumble and curse the May ;
The lime's one legion of smelling blossom,
  And hides her windows over the way.

TRAGEDIES.

SHE was a dancer,—I was her master ;
   Our troupe was rollicking on at the fair :
She and a stranger bit at one sweeting,—
A large pale-green one ripe for eating.
   (She has soft brown eyes and soft brown hair)—
'Twas down at the back of the booth, my sweeting,
   You never knew I was there !

My brain was fire.   At fall of night,
   By a great black cedar, dagger'd dead,
She lay, turn'd clear to the wind's quick cries,
In the long grass writhing with flamed fire-flies,
   And the white stars shrinking, high overhead.
And he was dreaming of paradise,
   In a laughing wanton's bed !

Tragedies.

SHE reach'd a rose-bud from the tree,
  And bit the tip and threw it by:
My little rose, for you or me,
  The worst is over when we die !

My little love, my lily wan,
  Of life so weary, weep on me !
Come lay your head, and on, and on,
  I'll ripple low love-tales to thee !

In calm white moonlight sleeps the swan,
  The reeds are wooing the willow-tree ;
Asleep and dreaming, on, and on,
  I'll drift you into the endless sea !

And I was a full-leaved, full-bough'd tree,
 Tranquil and trembling, and deep in the night,
And tall and still, down the garden-ways
 She moved in the liquid calm moonlight.

Her moon-shot eyes, strain'd back with grief,
 Her hands clench'd down, she pass'd from sight ;
And I was a full-leaved, full-bough'd tree,
 Tranquil, and trembling, and deep in the night.

For love is like the China-rose
 That leafs so quickly from the tree ;—
And life, though all the honey goes,
 Lasts ever, like the pot-pourri.

Tragedies.

At top of the thinnest steeple-spire,
  Down below on the clattering square,
A carven angel with folded wings,
  And folded arms, and circling hair,
Looks on in everlasting prayer;
And down below the loud bell rings
From chime to chime; a swallow sings,
  A-building its nest in the belfry-stair;
  A grass-blade starts up here and there
And whispers and waves in the drafty air.

 ＊　　　　＊　　　　＊　　　　＊　　　　＊

A rose-set cloud had kiss'd her cheek,
  The gold-set sun had kiss'd her head;
Her wings were stroked by the pale twilight,
  The mart below was silencëd.
It chanced thereby an angel sped,
Belated in the coming night,
Who marvel'd at her forehead white,
  And marvel'd at her lips rose-red,
  And long'd to cherish her golden head,
And look'd, and long'd, and lingerëd.

And, thirsting at so tasty sight,
    Came nigh and touch'd her bosom-bed—

And shriek'd and started with affright,
    And upward, upward, sped and sped,
      For the carven angel was cold as the dead.

And the bar of heaven closes at night.

I DREAM'D I was in Sicily,
    All sky and hills and flowers;
We sat us under a citron-tree
    And courted, hours and hours.

I woke by the dunes of a bleak north-land,
    Along a lonely grave in the snow;
The salt wind rattled the ivy-band
    I 'd tied at the headstone long ago.

She was only a woman, famish'd for loving,
 Mad with devotion, and such slight things ;
And he was a very great musician,
 And used to finger his fiddle-strings.

Her heart's sweet gamut is cracking and breaking
 For a look, for a touch,—for such slight things ;
But he's such a very great musician,
 Grimacing and fing'ring his fiddle-strings.

———————

The river's mouth is weary wide,
 The banks are low as sight can see ;
Alone and sad, and side by side,
 We drifted on so tranquilly.

The white moonlight fell in a stream ;
 It silver'd her, it silver'd me :
Our thoughts wreathed out in a long love-dream,
 And mingled and melted over the sea.

In the middle of my garden-bed
  There stands a tall rose-tree ;
I took the stem and shook and shook it,
  Thick the flowers kept covering me.

And, oh ! I said, you sweet large roses,
  Red as rose can be,
Just drop into my bosom here,
  And die along with me !

In the warm wax-light one lounged at the spinet,
  And high in the window came peeping the moon ;
At his side was a bowl of blue china, and in it
  Were large blush-roses, and cream and maroon.

They crowded, and strain'd, and swoon'd to the music,
  And some to the gilt board languor'd and lay ;
They open'd and breathed, and trembled with pleasure,
  And all the sweet while they were fading away.

MAJOLICA AND ROCOCO.

I.

THROUGH God's great ether glows one sun,
  And one thrush pipes in the black, black grove ;
And deep in my heart, most one, most one,
  My love leaps out for thee, my love !

The sun sinks gold in Tethys' bed ;
  The rosy ether drops in the sea ;
The grove is still ; the thrush has fled ;—
  My whole soul overfloods with thee !

II.

WHAT master has so tuned her voice,
      That when she speaks,
Meseems some distant angel-choirs rejoice
      At some fair soul
That knocking entrance into heaven seeks ?

Is it her heart's a rebeck sweet?
    Who strokes the strings?
Unseen some glib-wing'd angel-paraclete,
    So sent of God
To fill my heart with heavenly hungerings!

III.

THE clear, fresh fount Hermaphrodite
    Was coying and kissing along with the sun,
Who caught it and kiss'd it to left and to right
In little glib drops of twinkling light,
Till quick to the ether's violet height
The rosy clouds, like snow-flakes light,
    Went wandering, melting one by one.

My lady and I, a long, long day,
    Were coying and courting the cloves among.
She kiss'd my love out, whither away!
Away and leagues in my soul away,
Where wandering fancies swirl and sway,
Away as in ether yet some day
    To shimmer to earth in a shower of song.

IV.

There's one great bunch of stars in heaven
   That shines so sturdily,
Where good Saint Peter's sinewy hand
   Holds up the dull gold-wroughten key.

There's eke a little twinkling gem
   As green as beryl-blue can be,
The lowest bead the Blessëd Virgin
   Shakes a-telling her rosary.

There's one that flashes flames and fire,
   No doubt the mighty rubicel,
That sparkles from the centre point
   I'the buckler of stout Raphael.

And also there's a little star
   So white a virgin's it must be ;—
Perhaps the lamp my love in heaven
   Hangs out to light the way for me.

v.

A PASTORAL.

FLOWER of the medlar,
    Crimson of the quince,
I saw her at the blossom-time,
    And loved her ever since !
She swept the draughty pleasance,
    The blooms had left the trees,
The whilst the birds sang canticles,
    In cheery symphonies.

Whiteness of the white rose,
    Redness of the red,
She went to cut the blush-rose-buds
    To tie at the altar-head ;
And some she laid in her bosom,
    And some around her brows,
And as she past, the lily-heads
    All beck'd and made their bows.

Scarlet of the poppy,
    Yellow of the corn,

The men were at the garnering,
   A-shouting in the morn ;
I chased her to a pippin-tree,—
   The waking birds all whist,—
And oh ! it was the sweetest kiss
   That I have ever kiss'd.

Marjorie, mint, and violets
   A-drying round us set,
'Twas all done in the faïence-room
   A-spicing marmalet ;
On one tile was a satyr,
   On one a nymph at bay,
Methinks the birds will scarce be home
   To wake our wedding-day !

VI.

WHEN I was by Chloe kiss'd,
Ceased or 'gan I to exist ?
If 'twas life before without her,
What is this to be about her ?

VII.

THE NAMING OF MY FAIR.

When night is come and lovers meet,
  And glow-worms all their lights have hung,
And nightingales sing killing sweet,
  Where erst the low-voiced loriots sung,—
I tune my lute at your window-bar,
And call you—My Star!

When dawn is white, and tipt with red;
  And, shouting 'mid the misty firs,
The shepherds leave their mountain-bed
  For pastures mad with grasshoppers,—
I wait you in your garden-way,
And call you—My Day!

When noon is over-hot and high,
  And viners loll the walls along,
And mountains melt in gauzy sky,
  And shrill cicalas whirr with song,—
I lay me in your lime's leaf-light,
And call you—My Night!

When twilight comes and tolls the bell,
 The bier winds slowly t'wards the church ;
The reapers wish the passer well,   .
 And stars come out and pigeons perch,—
I lay me where your love is rife,
And call you—My Life !

When day and all is dead and wail'd,
 And all's undone that might have been,—
In heaven's high music-room gargeyl'd,
 I scrape the quill to my mandoline.—
I'll time me where you read your scroll,
And call you—My Soul !

———————

VIII.

IF angels love above in heaven,
 Then death must be too oversweet ;
For this dear love thy lips have given,
 Has made this life, my love, replete.

IX.

O Hesperus a-gliding down the west
　　Close on the poppy-heads, with rosy wings,
And looking down the fields with clear large purple eyes,
　　　Hear the last song that sings
　　　　From my rent breast,
Ere the short day of love therein out-flies!

Hear it, and write along the burnish'd plate
　　Of the great sun, in letters of white gold,
That, as it wheels the slopes of mighty heaven round,
　　　The world may there behold,
　　　　And mark the fate
Of one a light lady has brought to ground.

X.

Sweet complement to every sense,
　　My flower, my fruit, my all that's fair,
My sum of God's munificence,
　　Thro' all the months that bud and bare;

Majolica and Rococo.

Thy cool hand's whiteness cannot wear,
   'Tho' mountain snows pulse out to sea ;
Their iris-becks bring no compare
   To those eyes mine would ever see
Thy tongue's the fragrant strawberry,
   Whence every cate and junket gains ;
Thy breath's aroma, marjory,
   Could cordial even lovers' pains ;
And eke thy lips such rhetoric make
Nightingales die for envy's sake.

XI.

THE GUILD OF HER BEAUTY.

WHAT cunning craftsman coin'd the thread
   Of gold her hair so fair and fine?
What gardener laid her bosom-bed
   Where long her lily arms entwine?

What dyer such rich red has wrung
   For crimson of her lips and cheeks?
What master has so tuned her tongue
   To make such music when she speaks ?

What alchemist has blown her breast
  To such a white quick leap of fire,
That when I lay me there to rest
  I'm all consumèd with desire?

————————

XII.

AUBADE.

When fair Hyperion dons his night attire,
  Purple and silver, and his eyes with sleep
  Go trembling, and the lids a-kissing keep,
And up he wings the plains of heaven the higher,
  The starry meadows all uncurl and creep
  With twinkling shoots that tremble out and leap
From buds into a blossoming of fire.

When Spring, with primrose-fillet round her brows,
  Drifts on the dawn into the hyacinth west,
  And flings fresh handfuls hoarded in her nest
Of tasty flowers, to Flora making vows,
  The snow leaps down the mountain-side, and, press'd
  With weight of leaves, the earth at happiest
Rills into rivers thick from blossom-boughs.

When Liris comes sometime at break of day
    To take the vervain-garlands from the door,
    I've hung there fresh with dew an hour before,
And chances with soft eyes to look my way,
    My heart brims out with love, and crowding o'er,
    The passion-songs and rhythms spring and pour,
As storms in June or blossom-boughs in May.

XIII.

THE LOVE-TOKEN.

SHE has griffins twain to guard her gate,
    A mastiff-hound to watch in her hall,
A page for her train when she walks in state,
And minstrels and maidens around her to wait,
    And lovers and gallants at beck and call;
But ah! she left her shutter a-jar
For the cool to climb over the window-bar!

The griffins grinn'd in the moonlight green,
    The hound by the grim red embers slept;
I scraped a chord on my mandoline,

A chord, Pardè, that might ruin a queen !
And softly a-down the garden I crept ;
And, ah ! the song slid thro' the shutter a-jar,
And the lady lean'd over the window-bar !

XIV.

THE SUN OF MY SONGS.

THE birds are all a-singing,
The skies are mad with winging ;
And quick the seed-shells crackle, crickle, crackling up
the earth ;
The blossoms are thick in the trees,
The pleasance is crowded with bees ;
The fountain up-leaps, the anemones
Are shrill with the crickets in mirth.

And under her window I waited ;—
Alas ! she was still in bed !
My spring was all belated—
My sun is her golden head ;
And all my song
Was : " Ding, dong,

Summer is dead,
Spring is dead,
Winter is groaning along,
The birds are singing all wrong;
I would I were dead!"

From out her dreams she drifted,
The coverlet quick lifted,
And lithe her white-rose body uncurl'd from her snow-
white smock,
And tall at the window, and fair,
She combëd her golden hair,—
So fair—I would I were there, I were there,
To dazzle me dead in each lock!

"O madman, a dev'l to your dirging;
For spring's in the earth and the sky;
The rivers and meads are all surging
With red bud-coifs thrown by;
And every flower is shaking her head,
A-sheveling her hair on a green leaf-bed,
And making her comely and meet to be wed
Yet all your song
Is—' Ding, dong,
Summer is dead,
Spring is dead—

O my heart, and O my head !
Go a-singing a silly song,
  All wrong,
    For all is dead,
      Ding, dong,
    And I am dead,
        Dong !'

  .   .   .   .

"O gold my sun up-waking,
  Your curtain-clouds a-breaking,
Like runnels, rustling trees and merles, my songs out-sing
    your spring ;
  I'll sing of the warm blush-rose,
  And mellow the honey that flows
I' the bud that ripe to a full mouth blows,
Or white the bloom-blossom with love that glows,
And the gold-hair'd sun that makes me to sing.

"And yet to your honour I'll twine
  A garland fresh and fine ;
    And all the flowers that I shall pluck,
    The sweetest that bees suck,
Shall be these songs of mine.
  Oh ! such songs for me to sing,
    Ding, dong,
      Summer along,

And spring ;
All along, long life along—
After death they still shall sing,
Like to seeds of winter-thinking,
All their bud-shells crankle-crinking,
Shooting into summer song,
Bursting into blossoming."

XV.

THE PHIAL AND THE PHILTRE.

My lady has a casket cut
In scarlet coral, crimson-red ;
Like Cupid's bow, to keep it shut,
Two pouting locks are tightenëd,
In cunning curvings chiselëd.

Some mighty wizard it did make,
So strong that nothing can undo,
And if you thence would treasure take,
You press your lips the clasping to ;
The magic word's : "*I love but you !*"

You'll find a row of pearls within,
　As pure as scarce come from the sea,
And set the rose and crimson in,
　Twinkling with sweetest symmetry,—
　I trow most beautiful to see !

And eke the clasp's so cunning wrought,
　That as it opens, treble clear,
There comes a music, glib befraught,
　Like silver lutes, that to the ear
　As sweet love-ditties do appear.

And there within, as peach and rose,
　And pine and plum, most savoury choice,
Elixers sweet My Lady stows,
　To make the saddest heart rejoice,
　Or passionate the poet's voice.

A rich soul-philtre, that to sip
　I swear must be to drain it dry,
And never take away your lip
　Till time has toll'd your time to die,
　Yet dying love eternally.

XVI.

A GARDEN.

My love is red as oleander,
　And whiter than the rose,
And pure as never was such candour
　In any flower that grows,
And fresh and sweet as never was
The sweetness of azaleas.

If I might lie beside the bed
　Where all such shrubs do sprout,
And round my heart and soul and head
　Their virtues wreathe about,
Methinks the songs that thence would spring
Were meeter for my love to sing !

———————

XVII.

To love is but to live, my fair,—
　You would not surely have me die ?
So tangle my soul here tight in your hair
　Till I and you are only I.

XVIII.

The tulip to one blossom blows ;
　One ritournel the merles sing ;
My being with one great love glows,
　Whence all my fancies sprout and spring.

XIX.

A COURT-MINSTREL.

I dreamed I was a virginal,—
　The gilt one of Saint Cecily's ;
Her fingers, like sweet cordial,
　Went rilling and running along my keys ;
And round us, with their thin gold rings
　Above their heads, and clear calm eyes
Brimming with strange pure hungerings,
　The angels listen'd wondering-wise,
And press'd their white palms 'thwart the strings,
　To still their trembling psalteries.

I woke, Pardè, with a lute in hand,
　(My lady's the court courtesan :)

I'd slept, awaiting her command,
　For I'm My Lady's minstrel-man ;
And 'tis my task in the arbour-ring,
　Or at her chamber door, to wait,
And music light to make and sing,
　And hearts with pleasure to inflate
In time to the soft whispering
　Her lovers woo her with till late ;
To-night she sups my lord the King,
'Tis time I was a-musicking !

XX.

THE rose of her cheek may wane and die,
　Her hair's gold fibre dull and decay ;
But love has a colour not fused to fly,
　In the fabric that never shall wear away.

THE ANGEL OF GOD IN THE GARDEN OF DAME PHANTASY.

—⋆—

DAME FANCY's garden hath a deep bocage,
   Y-pleach'd of box and yew, in such smooth wise
It rather seems some plaster'd foliage,
   Round a stone gallery of quaint devise.
The gardener there hath also shown his wit
In florid arches; and the top as fit
To promenade all round, so broad is it,
   And lofty eke. straight up into the skies,
And spiss with little leaves could baffle Argus-eyes.

What time had Phœbus up his brilliant car
   Wheel'd to the pole, on chargers of white light,
A-nooning there the while on lands a-far
   He pour'd a spilth of Godship, as no wight
Can look on for the pureness of its shine,—

I did me in that umbrage cool incline,
And never thought nor cank'ring care was mine,
But just to sleep as long as well I might,
And to some Sylvan God anon my dreams indite.

I' the boughs around, with many pretty calls,
The birds were rhyming sonnets in love-chasse,
O'er multitudinous melodious falls
Around a fountain-base, where, wrought in brass,
A satyr held a plump wood-nymph at bay,
A-spirtling up the water every-way,
Right up pellucid, on me as I lay,
In rainbow mist, that on the green fresh grass
Did sprinkle little drops, twinkling like beads of glass.

And eke the sward was so thick set, and trim
With tender herbage, more as velouet
It seemëd,—smooth, to quite the basin-brim,
Where sylphs at the twelve cornices were set,
And quick within, a-flashing fro and to,
The crimson fishes swam, and the moss grew
With shining bubbles bright be-gemm'd, that thro'
The ripple-rings broke up, and half in fret,
Half laughter, like coy nymphs, their rims with kisses
wet.

I' the gentle draughts, flavour'd with flowers of clove,
  And full-blown roses ; lost in listening
To the sweet birds a-piping from the grove,
  And the fresh trickle of the fountain-spring.
I slumber'd on, and let my fancies clear
To run where'er they listed, till mine ear
Was struck by melody so sudden sheer
  That up I started, mad with marvelling,
To learn from whence it came, and question on the
    thing.

For such a music I had never heard :
  It was so passing pure, and rich withal
As never yet was pipe or treble bird,
  Nor gay, nor certes melancholial,
But sooner like a wight with a bird's soul,
Whose pleasure of itself is so sure whole
It hardly knows the virtues to condole
  Or grieve—yet hearts with feeling so to thrall,
As myriad nightingales trilling one madrigal.

And spying through a pleachèd arch of yews
  Down the long terrace, set with citron-trees
Of fruited fragrance, pied with all quaint hues
  Of flowers, and bosquets slumbèrous with bees

And flies a-shimmering in the burning noon,
Round every shrub, to every fancy hewn,
Or fowl, or cone, or griffin,—lo ! the tune
    Came from an angel thrumming at his ease,
And gliding down the sward as on the zephyr-breeze.

But could I you depaint the light that slid
    From fair his body, I had might of song
Like Orpheus, to bedazzle you unchid
    To very blindness ; for the walks along
That angel's glory flooded, crystal-pure,
A-rapturing every sense, I you assure,
With beauty, eyes and ears, as could endure
No mortal wight, yet in my brains among
Some cordial dropt from heaven and made them counter-
    strong.

So I could watch him, tall as a tall stem,
    With golden head thin-circled with a ring
Of metal bright as is no diamond gem,
    Nor gold, nor yet white flame ; and either wing
Just trembling softly through a crowd of eyes,
Like to a peacock's—gorgeous with dyes
Of green and gules all blending ; and like-wise
    His garment quaint was work'd with flower and ring,
On broad silk stripes like jewels burst in blossoming.

And 'mid his thick locks rilling from his head,
    Crisp as gold wires of god-craft, fine and small,
Around the auriole, or white or red,
    Roses were strung, and most ambrosial
The fan-winds piped, as closely to his back
His pinions shut in time ; till from the track
The air came trembling with low music, slack
    Where the soft rustle of his silken pall
The hem bestift with emeralds on the sward let fall.

But of his beauty, I can scarce essay
    To picture the white ivory and vermeil
Of curved his lips and cheeks ; or waved the ray
    Like down of rushes, each his eyebrows, pale
On broad his forehead, with the rings of gold
Circling a-down them ; or i' the loosen'd fold
His creamy throat a mystery to behold,
    With veins of violets and rose ; a tale
In each of beauty—yet to tell 'twould scarce avail !

Or eke the marvellous expression
    Of calm his eyes of grey, most tranquil hue,
That from the lash-fringe never brimm'd but on
    Gazed with a great still light, a-shining blue,
As from a very furnace of pure thought,

Where God had piled the fuel on, y-wrought
With trusting as with incense-savour ; taught
  Of Gabriel himself, so shrill and true
His voice from his round mouth, like flutes, rich rushëd
    through.

His mandoline he lean'd against his thigh,
  With outstretched arm, and with a flexile wrist
He scraped a gaudy quill he'd found thereby
  Along the silver twinkling strings, till whist
Each bird in piety, and from their bed
The flower-stalks curtsied, and the peacocks spread
Their plumes a-sparkling in the light he shed
  Around him, and I hearing hardly wist
If it was man or angel in me that did list.

At th' arbour entrance did he take his stand,
  Where thick and tall the stocks and lupins grew,
In time to the swift scudding of his hand
  The turnsols nodded round him in a row
As straight as a device up-till his waist,
And rush'd the runs and quavers in such haste
Of little sharp glib notes, in heavenly taste
  So florid—craving grace to word it so,
My ears seem'd dazzled quick as eyes with lightning-
    blow.

Then 'gan he sing of heaven and heaven's love,
    So every word or note a picture was
Most perfect, how the angel-saints above
    In that bright garden circling cycles pass
Of bliss and tranquil blessing and long days
In cool sequester'd grots, or clear the rays
Of God himself, flooding huge crowds that raise
    Majestic music in his great high mass
With lutes and clarinets and clashing cymbal brass.

Of calm clear dawns he sang, and evens eke,
    When jocund bands go forth to trim the stars
Jingling in tune to psalms of those that seek
    The purest soul-balms from the nenuphars
And lotus off the lakes of crystal light,
Or thyme-beds up the mountain-slopes bedight
With vapours soft as fruit-blooms, to the sight
    Stretching for myriad miles, and far, most far,
Flutt'ring with wingèd forms, fair as but angels are.

Or of the constant hearts that watch the door
    Where the souls enter, shading their strange eyes
Against the brilliant beauties that so pour
    Around them, lost in wonder, dazzling-wise.
Or calm the saints that wait, and watch, and pray,

With hungry brimming eyes for far away
Some lover lost in lechery, and gainsay
And spurn the pressing of such companies
Would turn or ease their thoughts with tender plea-
santries.

Or of the chamber of the blessëd mother,
With windows open, and the breath of clove
And sunlight drifting in, as each to other
The maidens tell sweet tales, and the time goes
From age to age ; and still they work and spin
Soft garments for the limbo, and whose sin
Was not their own, and ever mingling in
The music of some minstrel angel flows,
Who stands without, breast-high, 'mid the tall garden-
rows.

Of quiet orchard-closes fresh with spring,
The grass thick set with yellow crocuses,
And all the bared boughs white with blossoming,
And rich young green a-rustling in the trees,
Of which fond angel-lovers in the shade
Sit with their arms on either's shoulders laid,
Their heads upon their hands ; and man by maid
Read from one scroll unfolded on their knees,
And flooding in one time their thoughts with poesies.

Or when the ripe fruits rattle from the boughs,
　　Peaches and sweetings, and the leaves grow red,
And the torn rushes with the water-soughs
　　Go floating by where fruit 's ingarnerëd
To fill the press with luscious pulp and scent
Of pines and cloves.　The pious now intent
On sweet full-sugar'd wines for sacrament,
　　Against the autumn feastings, when each head
Is pamper'd round with trails of briony berries red.

Or of the rood-lofts of the still chapelles,
　　Where, lofty 'mid the steeple's oriel caves,
The thrushes building 'mid the chiming bells,
　　Carol clear songs ; and far below the sheaves
Are garner'd in on fields of stubble gold,
I' the golden sun, to where the set-cloud fold
Is pierced with rays along the purple wold,—
　　While ever rustle on the ivy leaves,
Stark to the yellow light the sunken sun still gives

Against the oriel frame-work, as one plays
　　Beside her gilt piped organ, 'long the keys,
In many runs and florid notes, and lays
　　Her head on one slim shoulder, and the breeze
Of evening whispers in her crisp gold hair,

Where marygolds are threaded ; and most fair
Her tap'ring fingers wander here and there,
  While all entranced at such sweet harmonies
A lover blows the wind-pipes, clinging to her knees.

Or of the crafty in the cool work-rooms,
  Broid'ring fair cloths and costly tapestries,
Minding the shuttle in the chuckling looms ;
  Or picturing missals with quaint phantasies,
And tales of holy writ, in trick and verse
So musical, that should a wight rehearse
With lips polluted, must bring direst curse ;
  For they are pure as the soft scents that rise
From those slight flowers that fade, if only suck'd by
    flies.

And many loving ways did he repeat
  In words and music so devotional,
That all my soul seem'd rushing head to feet,
  And feet to head, and every vein (how small,
No matter) in my body rang with pain,
From sheer excess of pleasure, to contain
Were past my strength—tho' ever had I fain
  Drink in with ears, into my very all,
Such healing sweeps of song, like balms ambrosial.

And feel some great God's presence most divine
  A-rushing through this dross of me, a wight,
Till well-nigh brent this weak body of mine,
  And let my soul run up to heaven's height,
A-drowning me the while in mandragore,
Till I nor knew nor heard, nor could restore
To any sense the power to question, or
  Examine into aught but the strange sight
Of song that in my soul flooded like Phœbus' light.

And when at last that angel's voice did cease,
  As with his thumb he set to tune the strings,
And all the world once more could breathe at ease,
  I stept forth, heartful of great questionings,
And said, with low and meet obeïsance :
" I crave the grace of your most high puissànce,
That I may ask if to your ears perchance
  The name of Lady Fancy, on the wings
Of fame, was ever borne 'mid other mortal things.

" For I avow, with all due deference,
  I honour'd am, tho' still her humblest swain,
To sing her praises, and with no pretence
  Pay her such humble homage can remain,
When minstrels, painters, jewellers, and also

All craftsmen, who of any culture know
Her tranquil influence, have striven to show
Her virtues ; nor have ever brought in vain
Their arts at her fair feet, her cognisance to gain.

" Withal as she is one who in good cause
Has work'd so nobly, and with such keen sense
Of God's great goodness,—eke and ever draws
Some farther use from his munificence,
Showing his might immense in every tit,
However small it seems to our small wit.
I crave that I might read of that fair writ
Whence come your songs, most gracious sir, and
hence,
In serving Phantasy, to God give preference."

To me the angel, with a tender look :
" Fond man, on this request to lay such stress !
For know one line y-writ in God's great book
But just to see, at your own littleness
'Twould be to perish,—all to atoms brent,
As spirit in thin flame to nothing spent,
Nor smoke, nor aught of which acknowledgment
Could ever be ; for if you know the less
Of heaven's beauty, 'tis to your own happiness.

" For poesy, as known to ye blind men,
     Is perfect heaven; but to us who see,
  'Tis God himself, whose mightiness we ken
     From line to line, to all eternity
  A-following his finger on the page
  Where all his beauty is y-writ, and rage,
  As mortals do, to reach the culminage
     Of his immeasured superiority,
To which we can but strain in flights of phantasy.

" Now of that heaven which we surely know,
     And ye but dream of—'tis the rose of love,
  The greatest gift that God doth but bestow
     In part to mortals, up their souls to move
  To heaven, where the whole will surely be;
  So as we dream God's beauty, so do ye
  Dream heaven's love, that God on every tree,
     Or flower, or cloud, or midge, has written so,
That learning ye might live, longing to further know.

" For eke in every form, and breath, and shade,
     A lesson of God's love is to be found;
  In every tit that he has plann'd or made,
     I' the meteor in the sky, or deepest sound
  Down in the earth its entrails 'tis y-writ.

But man, so blinded by his own conceit,
Must needs some paltry mortal counterfeit
　　Go grovelling at, intent upon the ground,
Whence back to his dull head his empty thoughts
　　rebound."

Whereon, as if the more to demonstrate
　　His words, he moved around his peacock-quill,
That with his hand such flashing did create
　　Of light, and eke so luminously fill
My poor weak eyes with glory, that there fell
As if a wimple from them, and most well
I saw the earth, fair as incredible,
　　Or through a crystal ball, where light did still,
Like crystal liquified by some great wizard's will.

For love was written each and everywhere,
　　Within, without that carven bocage pale;
In tiny wordings bright beyond compare,
　　E'en twinkling nights, when winter frosts unveil
Their white stars from all mist, and still above
The heavens loom, so dark and still, yet move
'T seemeth with myriad tremblings—so with love,
　　That garden breathed out gold, and glow'd vermeil
From every flower before—no matter how so pale.

And eke each herb and shrub—the crimson rose
    With pure soft silver letters was be-cinct ;
The lily-heads, spotless as virgin snows,
    Were blazon'd forth with red ; and interlink'd
Along the chalices, with flaming gold,
Were tinkling anagrams and rhymes enscroll'd
'Mid mazy borders ; maddening to behold,
    From sheer pleasaunce ; tho' yet my eyelids blink'd
At such conceits and words, and all so pretty prink'd.

The fountain on the sward in crystal drops
    Did tinkle out into an alphabet
Of letters like clear jewels ; and the tops
    Of the bocage, with the soft spray be-wet,
Twinkled with little gems like jingling bells ;
While from the sylvans in quick ritournels
The thrushes timed their quavers and sharp trills
    In beats of love, as bill to bill they met,
And read and told the tales on every leaf were set.

And eke from every daisy on the sward.
    And every herb, or blade, or gaudy bed
A vapour pure as incense curl'd and soar'd
    To heaven, above the highest poplar head,
In sweet straight spiralings, a-breathing prayer,

Religious, I trow, beyond compare,
And to the sight as most astounding fair
   As saintly to the sense—as when right said
Your soul in still chapelle with Christ hath communed.

I trow I was so lost in marvelling
   At this strange portent, more as one distraught
I ran about without the arbour-ring
   From flower to flower; yet, nathless, learning naught
Of what was there portray'd—but reading one,
Then th' other, ere the first was scarce begun;
Then to a third, and, ere that third was done,
   Unto a fourth, for the depicturing wrought
On each was of such beauty, 't seem'd it stopt my
     thought,

As pleasure caught my breath; and so my brain
   Went gasping, as it were, at each new trick
Of verse and wanton fancy; till contain
   Myself to one alone, were as if thick
In one small plum, I found the savouries
Of citrons, peaches, and ripe strawberries,
And wine, and honey of Hymettus' bees,
   And to the palate all things choleric,
Till like at one small read my brain grew surfeit-sick.

Yet eke so good found this new nourishment,
  Must tamper with it in extravagance
Of perfect plenty, as a toper spent
  With costly piments, still at his mischance
Goes tippling on, and flings away the draught
Ere yet the bubbles from the brim be quafft,
And shouts for more to fling away, berafft
  Of reason, in the sheer extravagance
Of pleasure, and so I with drunken looks askance

From every petal took a beauty drop,
  Like luscious liquor, till my silly head
With pictury, and rhyme, and thought, and trope,
  And music, was brimful replenishëd,
That surfeit labour thence could but accrue
From such variety of meats, tho' few
And choice, and chosen with attention due
  To the digesting, might have strengthenëd
My brain, till never yet was sage so letterëd.

This silly conduct when the angel saw,
  Y-seated on the fountain-brim, intent
Upon the twittering sweeps his quill did draw,
  A-tuning on his tight-strung instrument—
" O foolish man," quoth he, " who losest all

In trying to appease irrational
Thy weak desires, to rue and bitter gall
   Turning what God to thy salvation sent,
Thro' mad abuse, but to a well-timed chastisement.

" Nay, sooner choose, poor wight, some bud or rose,
   Or larkspur, yonder where so much is writ
Of beauty and divinement ; for who knows
   The best knows most ;—and to your benefit
Study it deeply, and the greater gain
Of wit will come, as you the more contain
Yourself unto one knowledge, tho' most fain
   To sluggard-man to thus neglect his wit,
And show instead some pompous empty counterfeit."

At these harsh words, come from so gentle source,
   I stood contrite enow ; and, thus dismiss,
And of my folly thinking have recourse,
   I pluck't one tall, white, spotless fleur-de-lis,
That from its spindle straight bow'd t'wards the east,
Letter'd and scroll'd with arabesques, at least
A thousand, wrought in gold, and inter-tress'd
   With purple-blues thro' the interstices,
With bold initials girt with tender imageries.

Whereon I found y-writ the blessèd love
  Of triply bless'd that maid immaculate,
Who, in her pretty parlour, sweet with clove,
  And fresh carnations in a red jar set
Beside the window, where, in a gilt cage,
Two doves were billing, fain received the gage
Of the Great Paraclete, reading her page
  Of daily prayer, as at her desk she sat
With one tall lily from her hand a-standing straight.

Around her virgin garment white and sweet
  Folded in great stiff folds, and by the door
A peacock strutted, and a-down the street
  The people flock'd to mass, and, arching o'er
From house to house, were stately balconies
In florid styles, set with great jars and trees
Of bushy green, thick with ripe oranges,
  And tapestries the ledges hung before,
And knights there courted dames that stately satins
    wore.

And eke how like sunlight and rings of gold
  She circled was by Saint Conception,
A-bending meekly as her did enfold
  The great God's presence, that so mighty shone,
The passers in the streets must shade their eyes,

The while a saint attendant in gay guise
Knelt in the close without, adoring wise,
  Light on the borders, where vermilion
And gold the tiny tulips trembled every one.

And as I fain would have re-read the rhymes,
  Their jingling trick and minstrelsy to know
To my heart's core, quick clatter'd out the chimes
  From pointed the mid palace tower; and lo!
The lily, and the angel, and the light
All vanish'd like a vision; and my sight
Bedazed and dazzled groped as in black night,
  And found me still along the fountain-flow,
Cadenced in slumbery music, trickling soft and slow.

But i' the clear sweep above of the great sky,
  Melting from saffron pale to violet,
Sweet Hesperus like a jewel twinkled high
  In calm still light, against the which close set
The bosquet trees stood outlined black and square
As eke the statues by the terrace stair
All open to the twilight, where in pair
  The fireflies glimmer'd faintly, and, just wet,
The air was sweet with lush heart's-ease and mignonette.

And down the terrace came the sweeps of lutes,
 And whispering, and soft footfalls rustling by,
And trailing robes, and clarinets, and flutes,
 As soft as could be heard, and minstrelsy
Most meetly as Dame Phantasy doth chuse
On summer even's, when it is her use
To pass to this bocage, and 'mid the yews
 Spend a calm hour in goodly company
Of such fair knights and ladies love her courtesy.

So I up-rose and hurried, still intent
 On my strange dreams, to meet her in the way,
A-gathering such posies as I went
 Had figured there ; for, ere they quite decay,
Methought, I'll bring them to Dame Phantasy
Herself, whose knowledge keen may there descry
Some traces of the tricks and pictury
 I fancied were y-writ ;. and if she may,
The simples of her art will make them live alway

THE END.

www.ingramcontent.com/pod-product-compliance
Lightning Source LLC
Chambersburg PA
CBHW020623030726
47497CB00007B/2383